The Mafia Man
Through the Eyes of a Criminal

by Christopher Kenneth Patton

RoseDog Books
PITTSBURGH, PENNSYLVANIA 15238

RoseDog Books
585 Alpha Drive, Suite 103
Pittsburgh, PA 15238
Visit our website at *www.rosedogbookstore.com*

ISBN: 978-1-4809-8354-0
eISBN: 978-1-4809-8331-1

Introduction to the book

What if it were possible for you to be a real mafia man? What does it take to be an organized criminal that never gets caught? Would you like to be able to do whatever you want no matter what? The answer to these questions is probably yes to some and no to others. From narrow escapes with the law to the high-class living this kind of lifestyle can pay for, in this book you will meet a mafia man named Rick Thompson and you will experience just what an organized criminal can do. Maybe you will find out if you can succeed as a career criminal or maybe you will find out that you cannot ever do anything like it. If you have decide that you are not mafia material then let's hope this story keeps you at the edge of your seat and keeps you suspended in the lifestyle of a professional conman.

Table of Contents

The Mafia Man

Chapter 1

Who am I? Well, I'll tell you who I am. I happen to be the best mafia man you've ever seen in your life. The name is Rick, Rick "The Slick Man" Thompson and there is more than one reason for the nickname. Firstly, I am the only mafia man that never gets caught, I'm slippery as a snake. Second, it's also after the way I grease back my all-black hair with silver highlights by using too much hair gel. The question you need to ask yourself is just what a real mafia man and his profession really are. Most people would say organized crime and I would come back with the question for them to define "crime" and the term "criminal". I would also add in, "Is what I do wrong or immoral?" If you answer the question with a "yes" then, I would ask you if you know what a real mafia man does in this drab and depressing society with a blue, melancholy appearance and feel. If I decided I could trust you and it is worth my time and money then I could introduce you to society's underworld, where the misfits of society loom.

Besides the super-rich of this empty existence, it is the underworld where my unacceptable deeds make my loot. But how as a mafia man do I pay my dues? I will tell you. Potions, I sell potions and some will claim that potions are a sin, not to mention illegal. Oh well enough of me introducing myself.

However, in this world of empty dreams and the establishment by the powerful on this planet, you need to know how this world turns its wheels.

A lot of secrecy by the Catholic government runs through the wealthiest via religious intuitions and a hierarchy of churches. It is usually true that most of the religious practitioners in this society are of the Catholic faith. This used to always be true about a mafia man as well. He was always a Catholic man, but now we follow a different idea with spirituality. The usual decision on a mafia man's faith now almost always follows *Man's Book of The Law*. The religion within the pages of this book is known as LaVeyan Satanism. "What is LaVeyan Satanism?" you might ask. To tell you the truth, the religion is about doing whatever you want to do, but only if it benefits you or someone else. It is true about a real mafia men that we spend all our time doing evil deeds to benefit someone else's life. So yes, we help people. I happen to help people by giving away money, which is why, once a month, I try to give away twenty-five thousand dollars.

They always call someone who was born into a mafia family a natural-born gangster, but only if they decided to be in the mafia. It has been a secret in these families for generations on how to train and excel at being a gangster, but for good reasons.

Are there other mafia men out there besides me? The answer to this question is yes, but I never work with them. A real good mafia man only works by himself. This is because he always is good enough to always get away with all of it.

This tavern where we are drinking at right now in this yellowish dimmed light is my favorite hotspot to relax at and partially avoid the local law enforcement. They don't always come to the bad side of town in Greens City, the biggest city you can find.

This dirty rat that I am onto for following me is sitting over there in the corner by himself. I haven't figured him out as a snitch quite yet, but if he comes to close to me I will take him out at home and ditch his body in the woods or maybe make it look like he hanged himself. I am not sure how violent I want to be with him for pissing me off as a snitch. I will tell you one thing, I hate a snitch, and Johnny Law can't do anything about it because of the way I operate. I don't get caught. Although I will tell you what, the law isn't as good at being the law as they want people to believe or I would be sitting in the big house for all the bad things I have done.

Even though I realize it is sick of me to kill a man for my own good reasons, especially with the huge amount of torture and violence I may decide to use for fun, I still try not to care about it at all. Good mafia men learn to not give a damn about anything they do so they learn to ignore their emotions and conscience. Yes, we do whatever we want no matter what, even though helping people as a mafia man is the real point of the job. There happens to be another reason to be in the mafia and the other purpose is having fun, because it is supposed to be fun.

If you are going to be in the mafia then you should always find a wife that doesn't mind your occupation and keeps her trap shut about your work. It is also usually a good idea to maybe knock your wife up a few times. Then you look like a decent family man.

It is usually true that the law knows what you do for a living but for some reason your neighbors never find out anything. I guess it's because the government never tells anyone anything that they know about you. Who knows why they keep their mouths shut.

"Well bartender," Rick said in a loud voice, "Can you add up my tab now that I am done relaxing, so I can get home to my beautiful wife before she wonders why I didn't come straight home after the one job I had today?" The job I had today was making a large and expensive delivery of my goods.

The bartender walked over to his 1940s brand-new cash register, tallied up my two drinks, and then gave me the bill. I then reached into my back pocket, grabbed my wallet, and took out a one dollar bill to pay for the drinks, which were a total of fifty cents. The bartender walked back over to the cash register and pulled out two twenty-five cent coins. The bartender then handed the two coins to me. I nodded goodbye and started walking to the front door of the tavern. I stepped out of the tavern onto the front sidewalk outside the drinking establishment, turned right, and started walking to my 1943 pickup truck. I bought this truck new about six months ago from the car dealership in downtown Green City. I unlocked the driver's side door with the key and then I took my seat behind the steering wheel. I then placed the key into the ignition and proceeded to start the automobile's engine. It started with a small roar. I backed the truck up onto the busy street behind me, shifted the truck into first gear, and drove home to see my wife and family.

When I got home, I realized that my wife's car was not parked in our two-stall garage. That is when I looked at the time on my diamond-encrusted gold watch. It took me a minute to realize my children's school day had just ended so she might be picking them up after their long day of learning. I finished parking, turned off the engine, then closed the garage door and walked into my house. I owned a home on Everette St in a somewhat wealthy neighborhood. I could own a house like this because the potion business was good to me.

I then proceeded to walk to my bedroom upstairs. When I went into it, I randomly picked some looser-fitting clothes from my closet and changed out of my suit. After I changed my clothes, I went down to the family room, turned on our radio, and started to listen to my favorite station. Then I grabbed myself a glass of scotch on the rocks to sip on.

After I relaxed for about twenty minutes, I heard a car pull into our drive-way. I looked out my front window and it was the worst of all criminals pulling up into my driveway. Paul "The Pimpled Pimp" was exiting his vehicle and walking to my front door. I was not looking forward to talking to this smelly, fat, and ugly existence. Did he have pimples? The answer is usually yes. He was the most disgusting creature you'd ever meet. No one ever handles the yellow stench fuming from his body, not to mention his disgusting manner-isms. Bad habits like picking his nose in public or scratching his behind for ev-eryone to see. You usually ask yourself when did he last shower. The only reason a woman ever decided to talk to him was because he paid them to and he claims they make him look good. I don't know how Paul can think he ever looks good.

I heard him knock on my door and I cringed as I opened it.

Paul said hello to greet me and then asked, "Have you seen Jennifer Nic-olson?" She was his most popular working girl.

I replied with, "Why do you think I would have seen her?"

He somewhat snapped back, "Because she is one of your best customers which is something I do not enjoy out of her or you."

I thought about it and remembered I had seen her last week, Tuesday, when she came to my house and made a rather large purchase of potions. I answered his question by saying, "I happened to talk to her last week sometime. Maybe Tuesday was the day she was here."

Paul then asked, "Why was she at your residence?"

I answered with the truth and told him, "She was here to buy my intoxicating goods."

He also decided he would ask me, "Do you know where she would be after she bought the trash you sell?"

"No, she didn't mention anything about where she would be," I answered.

Paul then asked me, "If you see her again sometime soon, would you let me know?

My answer to this question was, "Yes, I will do what I can."

He thanked me, left, and I acknowledged him with a, "your welcome" and "goodbye".

About another five minutes after Paul left, the front door opened and my wife and three children walked into the house. I stood up from my easy chair to hug my wife and three children. I have two girls and one boy. The oldest is Theresa, the one in the middle is Darren, and the youngest, the boy, is Kyle.

My wife greeted me, "Hello, darling."

I answered back with, "How was your day Linda?"

She said, "It was kind of boring really."

Sometimes her day would be this way since she did not have any formal employment. I was the only one in the house who brought home any type of paycheck.

Linda then asked me, "Did anything happen exciting in your day?"

I replied with, "I made one big sale of about seventy-five hundred dollars."

Linda was happy to hear it because she then asked me about something she had been wanting for a while and said, "I have been thinking about buying a greenhouse to have a small garden in."

"Where do you want it to be at?" I asked my wife Linda.

She answered with, "Right in the middle of the backyard."

I said, "Okay, maybe this weekend we can go shopping downtown and see what we can find."

Later that evening, my wife cooked diner and made one of my favorite dishes of hers which was lasagna. After my family had dinner, my children finished their homework which I made them do, and they had to do a good job on it. After they were finished with their homework, I sent them to bed with a snack and told them, "Good night."

In the morning, at six-thirty, I awoke to my alarm clock beeping at me, telling me it was time to get up. I pulled myself together and stood up out of bed, wishing it wasn't time to get up already. My wife was already up and trying to get our children ready for school. Meanwhile I was trying to remember what I had to do today. I then remembered, I had to get a lot of money together, which I did have, then see the chemist that brews up my potions so I can make a purchase that was probably around the one hundred thousand dollar mark.

I went into the kitchen after I crawled out of bed and said, "Good morning" to my wife and three children.

I got dressed for the day, I ate a small breakfast, grabbed my car keys, and then made my way outside to my automobile. I drove down to my bank to make a sizable withdrawal. I slowly pulled into the bank's parking lot, got out of my car, and then walked through the front doors of the bank.

I approached the teller inside the bank and I asked, "Can I withdraw one hundred thousand dollars?"

The bank teller, who was a woman, declared, "You must talk to the head banker about a withdrawal of that size." She then brought me to the banker's office and said, "Just talk to him and he will be able to assist you."

I told the banker, "I would like to withdraw a lot of money."

The banker said, "How much?"

I told the banker, "I want to withdraw one hundred thousand dollars."

He said, "Okay, let me see your account balance and I will be right back." He left the office and looked at the paper work for my savings and checking accounts. "Okay, you do have the money to make this withdrawal," the banker explained. "If you would like I can access the bank vault and the return with your money."

"That would be fine," I declared.

The banker replied, "Okay, I will be right back with your transaction."

About five minutes later the banker returned with a stack of one hundred dollar bills and handed them to me. I reached out, grabbed ahold of the money, and stood up then I walked out of the bank with my withdrawal. Now that I had my dough it was time to go see Robby Robinson, who was the ultimate potion brew master. Robby is one of crimes wealthiest because not very many gangsters thought it's fun to cook something so dangerous. Not to mention how much the law wants to punish someone who is a source for organized crime.

As I pull up to Robby's house, I noticed that his basement windows were covered from the inside, which usually meant he was busy doing what he does for the underworld of gluttony. He must have seen me pull up and get out of my vehicle because as soon as I made it to the front door it opened with Robby's sunk in and strung-out face. It was usually obvious to us criminals that Robby really did love potions, which was probably why he made such terrible things in the first place.

When I walked up to the brew master and he said in a strange way, "Who are you and what do you want?"

I said to Robby, "You need to back up off all of the potion and get yourself straightened out. I am Rick and we kind of know each other."

"Oh yeah, that's fine. It's Slick Rick. I'm sorry, I didn't recognize you."

I then asked, "Could I come in and do some business?"

"Shh shh shh," he hissed at low volume. "If my neighbors hear that, the fuzz will show up," he exclaimed. "I am busy creating what I do best right now and so there is no way to cover this up," he whispered.

"Okay, I'll shut up," I said in a low voice. "Just let me in, you loose screw."

He opened the door just far enough to let me in and I slid through the crack he left. I proceeded to slam the door and looked through the peephole with nothing but paranoia for the church-going government.

After paranoid Floyd finished letting me into his home, I questioned him by saying, "What do you have for good times?" I was somewhat disappointed with his answer because I had a lot of customers right now.

Robby replied by telling me, "Not much, which is why I am working right now. So maybe you can come back tomorrow?"

I unhappily stammered with, "What do have available right now?"

He said in rude voice, "Nothing at all right now. So you just have to come back tomorrow and I will have what you want."

"Fine," I shot back at him and then asked, "Will you have one hundred thousand dollars' worth?"

I wasn't happy with his next remark which was, "No, I can only have about half that much."

"Well, if you are going to short me like this, can you make sure I have at least half of what I want when I come back tomorrow?"

"I got you covered," Robby said in a loud voice. "Oh, and have you heard, now that its spring time with nature coming back to life from winter, there is a chance for some cherry apples to be found in the Birchwood forest?" Robbie was excited to find out if it is true.

Cherry apples have been around for some time. They are the most potent potion that is known to man and they exist naturally, I eagerly thought.

"This plant is always destroyed by the government if they find one during the summer and that has been why you don't find the cherry apple for sale in the fall when they are ready for the harvest," Robby said in an unhappy manner. He then added, "There were a few of us professionals in our trade-craft, you know. We are trying to think of a way to protect this plant from the churches and higher powers like the government."

"Well, I don't know how to get this one done and get away with it, so we don't get caught red-handed and then have to pay for that one, you know, le-gally," I said this back to Robby. "I will just let myself out" I said back to Robby. I walked back to my truck, got in, and drove home since there was no reason for me to be out doing business.

By the time I made it home it was about two thirty in the afternoon and I thought about what to do with the rest of my day. I decided it was too early to start drinking so I put that idea to the back of my mind. I decided to pick up the house and spend some time cleaning, which was usually my wife's job. I was doing this because my wife had business outside the home, grocery shop-ping and buying some other things downtown that we needed.

I asked her on her way out the door, "When will you be back?"

"For as long as it takes me to buy an iron, a coffee maker, and some groceries."

"Alright, well hurry back then," I told her as the door was closing.

I spent the next two and a half hours cleaning, mostly with a feather duster. By that time, my wife came home and since it was Friday night and about five o'clock, I decided to get stinking drunk. I walked up to the liquor cabinet in the kitchen and grabbed a full bottle of bourbon. I then proceeded to pour a cocktail glass up to the brim and served it over four square ice cubes. I spent my night drinking until probably eleven o'clock, by then I was intoxicated enough to stop drinking. I placed my glass, which was now empty, in the sink and made my way to bed for the night. My wife was already asleep and I think maybe I upset her by trying to get into bed drunk. As I was falling asleep I thought, *I am going to be sick tomorrow.*

I had been up for a while this morning and regretting the night before, especially when my wife showed me the glass snow globe I had broken in my drunken stupor the night before. She was really upset about me breaking her snow globe because her dying mother gave it to her on her death bed. Her mother received it from her mother when she was on her death bed and then it was gifted to my wife. I wasn't quite sure how to apologize for this one or make up for it, aside from letting my wife yell for half an hour.

I explained to my wife that I don't know what to do about it aside from saying, "I am sorry."

"Well that's not good enough!" she yelled.

That was about the end of the lecture I got from her.

A couple of hours after my wife's lecture, I decided to maybe get some work done by going over to Robby's house and making a big purchase. This way I could make some money on Monday and make sure my customers have what they need. I grabbed the stack of cash I took from my bank account and got into my truck to drive to Robby's.

Robby once again saw me pull up into his driveway and he was at the door by the time I had gotten to it and the door was open. I walked in to Robby's house and closed the door behind me.

After I walked into Robby's house he told me, "It went a little faster making potions than I expected and I do have one hundred thousand dollars' worth to sell."

I handed him the cash, everything I withdrew. After I paid him, we loaded the potions into the back of my truck. We placed a black plastic tarp over it and used elastic bands to secure it down so no one could tell what was in the back of my truck.

"Good bye and thank you," I said to Robby and he replied the same. I started my truck with the key and proceeded to go home.

When your trafficking potions that are illegal, you want to make sure you follow all traffic laws so you don't get pulled over by the law and get caught. As I was on my way home, I passed an officer of the law. I was not speeding or breaking any laws, but he knew my business and was trying to look at what I was transporting. I didn't get pulled over, but I am pretty sure he couldn't tell what was in the back of my truck. I may have got somewhat lucky this time because I think he was in the middle of something. It looked like he was busy already because someone was in the back seat and the warning lights were on.

When I got home I pulled completely into my garage and made sure I pulled the big garage door closed all the way to the ground and I locked it shut. I thought I needed to make my move and hide these illegal goods quick since there was an officer parked just down the street, probably watching me. I immediately started moving all of the potion to the basement. I have a hidden vault in the floor where I keep these types of things and it is really hard to find. My wife and kids were back from shopping by the time I got home from Robby's and she was starting to cook dinner.

I asked, "What are we having for dinner?"

My wife replied, "We are having a roasted chicken and garlic mashed potatoes."

It was about an hour and a half after dinner and my wife had just finished doing the dishes when Jennifer Nicolson knocked at my door.

I opened the door, said "hi" to Jennifer, and told her, "Paul was over here looking for you the other day and asked me if I have seen you and to let him know if I did."

"Oh well, actually I was out of town at my sister's wedding," Jennifer claimed.

I then asked, "Well, do you want to go tell Paul you are home?"

"If you could give me a ride over there then that would be fine," she answered. "Also, could I buy some potion while I am here?"

That is what I assumed she wanted when I saw her at my door, but I was fine with that and asked her, "How much?"

She said, "I have fourteen dollars to spend."

"Well right now it is two dollars per dose," I explained.

"Okay, I will take seven doses." When she said that I could sort of that tell she had been without any potion for quite a while being out of town at a wedding.

I told her, "Step inside, close the door, and wait for me to get what you are asking for." I went down to the basement, grabbed what she wanted, and then went back upstairs and gave her the merchandise.

She looked at it and said, "This looks fine, so here is the payment," and she handed me fourteen dollars.

"Now just let me go and grab my automobile keys and I can take you to see Paul, if that is what you still want?" I was sort of asking.

Jennifer said, "Yes we might as well."

We went out to the garage and I opened the big garage door and then we both sat down in the truck. I started it up backed up on to the road and started driving to Paul's house.

We pulled up in front of Paul's house, which happened to be a twenty-five-minute drive across town. It was starting to get dark outside, it wasn't all that late but there were no lights on inside Paul's house. We both decided that we would knock anyways so we walked up to the big front door. I grabbed ahold of the heavy brass knocker and slammed it against the door three times. We waited about five minutes and tried the knocker again about two minutes later. We decided to leave since no one was answering the door.

We were almost back to the car when we heard the door open and a loud, "What do you want?" in Paul's voice from the front door.

Jennifer yelled back, "I heard you were looking for me," as we both walked back up to the now open front door.

He couldn't make out who we were in the dark and so he squinted his eyes and said, "Well who are you?"

Jennifer answered back, "It's me, Jennifer Nicolson, and Slick Rick is here with me. He was my ride over here."

"Oh good, Jennifer is here," Paul said in a groggy fashion. "Well, I had asked Rick if he saw you to let me know and it looks like he did that. Good, I am happy he got you over here."

I asked Paul, "Why are all of your lights off?"

He replied, "The same reason it took me so long to get to the front door, I was asleep. But I am awake now so you might as well come in, that's if you want to."

As soon as I and Jennifer walked into Paul the Pimpled Pimp's house, I took one breath and realized were I was at. I was at a house that made me somewhat gag from breathing in the noxious scent that followed Paul everywhere.

Paul then asked Jennifer, "Where have you been? You better have a good reason because you are losing me money."

She answered the question with the same answer she gave me. "I was at my sister's wedding out of town," she said.

"Well fine, but you should have told me where you were going since I am your employer. Just make sure you're ready for work tomorrow," Paul added. "When I was at your place the other day I was thinking, could you be hired to do some dirty work for a friend of mine?" Paul asked.

I could tell he didn't want to ask but did anyways.

Paul explained, "He is a thief, which kind of makes him the lowest of the low when it comes to criminals."

Paul is kind of right, thieves are the worst and you can't trust them at all because they will rob their own mother if it's going to make them some money. The bottom line is there is nothing they wouldn't take.

I asked Paul, "What's the job?"

Paul quietly said one word, "Murder".

I stated, "Okay, so you want someone taken out?"

"Yeah," Paul grumbled, "And I will tell you who if you will do it."

I replied, "I don't usually do wet work unless I absolutely have to," I explained to Paul. "The problem is that it is hard to get away with, even though I do like the thrill of the kill and the smell of the bloodshed."

What just came out of my mouth sounded sick in the head, I was thought.

"The job pays two hundredthousand dollars, if that makes you change your mind," Paul mentioned.

I was thinking to myself, *Maybe this one is worth it with that price tag.*

I decided to ask, "Who do you want snuffed out?"

"An eye witness to a burglary and murder in my friend the thief's legal case. He got a little bit caught for this one," Paul stammered out.

"So how did he get caught?"

"He had decided to rob a house and in the middle of it the man who owned the house, Patrick Bensy, came home. The man who owned the house attacked my friend the thief. Right before Patrick physically got to him, the thief pulled out a knife and stabbed the man to death. The man started to scream as he was stabbed and the neighbor heard the commotion. When the neighbor looked out the window, she saw the thief fleeing out the back door, hoping he would not be caught for this. Anyways, this is what the neighbor said to the police when being questioned. She got a good look at him and gave a decent description." This was the short story Paul gave to me about the hit.

"One more question Paul, what is the thief's name and why haven't I heard of him in the area, if he is a known criminal?"

"He just moved into Greens City about six months ago and hadn't started operating in the area until about one month ago," Paul answered. "He moved here to try to lose the heat he had on him from the local police in the last place he lived at. To answer your other question on his name, it is Stan Sowersworth. He also mentioned that the people he knew in the place he lived at before here called him 'Sticky Fingers Stan'. Stan is also the man that will pay you to do the evil deed."

I said, "The last thing I need to know is, who am I going to do in?"

Paul replied, "Her name is Eleanor Wilson and let me see… I have her address around her somewhere."

As Paul started looking around for the address, I glanced at my watch and knew I should get myself home. It's getting late.

Jennifer who was still there asked Paul, "Could I stay the night here?"

Paul then said, "Here it is, Eleanor's address already written down for you Rick and yes, Jennifer, you can stay the night on that couch over there."

Jennifer said, "Thanks Paul."

Paul handed me the address and also remarked, "I will let Stan know the job will get done. That's if you decided to take the job?"

"Yes, let Stan know I will help him out." I added, "I will get it done tomorrow night."

Paul exclaimed, "Alright, I will let Stan know we have this one taken care of!"

As dusk moved in the day after I told Paul I would off someone for him, I was contemplating what I was about to do to someone who was probably completely innocent.

It was six o'clock in the evening. I was having dinner with my family and my wife asked, "Why are you so restless?"

I said, "Well, I have a rough job tonight. If you want to know what it is, let us walk into the other room away from our kids."

"Okay, fine," Linda said and then also remarked, "If it's like that I would prefer not to know. We will just finish eating dinner and you can go about your business." Linda finished what she was saying with this comment and then stayed silent for the rest of our meal.

I could tell that sometimes maybe she wished she hadn't married a mafia man.

Chapter 2

It's getting late now. The sun is completely down and it is one o'clock in the morning. This is late enough to get away with murdering Eleanor Wilson. This way Stan's murder case goes the way he needs it to go.

I grabbed my hand gun, a decent-sized combat knife, some gloves to not leave finger prints, a ski mask to cover my face, and a long piece of rope. I had all this set out on the table for tonight. I put it all in a burlap sack and left my home in my pickup truck and started driving to Eleanor's house.

As I was pulling up to Eleanor's place, I noticed all her lights were off inside her home and there was no porch light on in front of her house. I thought, *Good, no one can see me walk up to her house.*

I parked my truck about one block away, stepped out of it, and shut the door as quietly as I could. I covered my face with the ski mask, put on the gloves, and sneakily walked up to Eleanor's front door.

Now I needed to make sure I can secure Eleanor in her home, so this way she couldn't run for help and scream. I first tried the front door. It was locked and I decided to take my chances of her neighbors seeing me.

What I did was knock on her door to wake her up and it worked, because I saw a light turn on through the window upstairs. She eventually made her way to the front door. As soon as the door opened, I pulled my pistol, pointed it at Eleanor, and then pushed her into her front room.

I told her, "Shut up or you die," while I forced my way into her home.

I opened the burlap sack I had in my other hand and grabbed the rope. I made sure it was a brand-new rope and did not have any traces from me on it. I gave the rope to Eleanor and told her, "Hold on to that rope for a while so I can think."

She did not know I was plotting a way to get her finger prints on the rope without mine or anybody else's. I was planning on getting away with this by making it look like a suicide. The method I decided to use would be hanging, even though I am making it look like she hanged herself. This was what the government is supposed to believe. Even though I am the one that is going to hang her, it is still the way she will die. I looked at the ceiling, looking for a place to hang the rope, and I decided to tie the noose onto a light fixture with a fan on it that was suspended in kitchen.

I placed my hand gun in the back of my pants as Eleanor was deathly frightened and begged, "Don't hurt me. Take whatever you want."

I grabbed the rope from Eleanor and began tying a hang noose. After I tied the noose to the light fixture, I placed a chair under it for her to stand on. I then forcefully grabbed the woman I was killing tonight and stood her on the chair, placed the noose around her neck, and... *SLAM!* I kicked the chair out from under her and she began to hang. She was flopping around like a fish out of water, not handling her breath being cut off. About twenty minutes later she had finished dying and obviously none of her neighbors saw anything because no police showed up.

I looked around to make sure my tracks were covered at the crime scene and I did not notice anything. I took my gun, knife, mask, burlap sack, and gloves with me as I left her house in the dark. The only thing left behind was the rope. I sneakily walked back to my truck and opened and closed the door as quietly as I could while I got in. I started up the engine and drove back home.

There was no one awake at my house when I got home. I slowly made my way to the door, trying to make as little noise as I could so I didn't wake up my family. I opened the door to a few members of the street gang called The Galt Gang and they immediately asked me "Can we buy some potion?"

The Galt Gang was not a mafia because they just weren't organized enough. But they could be a problem for anyone with the amount of hell they raise in public. They sometimes buy a decent amount of potion because they like to sell it after they buy it from me. They make money because it's cheaper to buy large amounts of potion. I give a sale price for large orders at one dollar per dose instead of two dollars per dose.

Since I was up and had0 plenty of potion right now, I asked these Galt Gang members, "How much potion do you want?"

They came up with the question, "How much can we get for ten thousand dollars?"

I told them, "My potion usually goes for two dollars per dose so you normally would get about five thousand doses. However since you are buying this much, I will sell it to you for one dollar per dose. Which comes up to ten thousand doses for the amount of money you have."

They were talking in front of me to decide if that was what they want and they decided. "Let's just spend it all and buy as much as we can," one of the gang members remarked.

I usually tell customers to bring something to put it in so I asked, "Did you bring something to put it in, say a couple of duffle bags?"

They made the remark, "We did forget to bring something to put it in this time, so hmm… what can we do about it?"

"If it's fine with you," I asked, "I could put it in plastic garbage sacks?"

"That would be just fine," they told me.

I went and opened the kitchen cupboard, grabbed the box of garbage bags, and removed four full size bags. I went down to my basement and opened the vault in the floor where my potions were at and then counted out ten thousand doses, which took about an hour and a half. I filled the garbage bags full of potion and went back upstairs.

"Here you are," I said as I handed them the potion. They in turn handed me ten thousand dollars, nodded their heads goodbyes, and left out through the door.

I heard them start their automobile and drive away as I was making my way to bed after kind of a late night. Being sort of self-employed, I can sleep in whenever I want. So a late night doesn't bother me too much.

The morning after, I woke up and I was going through what I needed to do. I had decided I would go to Paul's house and tell him I had murdered the witness in Stan's murder case. After arriving at Paul's house, we went over what I had done the night before to make sure I wouldn't be caught.

Paul said, "I have a guy that is going to watch the house, so we know when the cops have discovered the body." Paul then wanted us to go get into his automobile and drive to the thief Stan's house and tell him what had been done and give him the chance to pay me for what I did for him.

When we arrived at Stan's house, I was kind of eager to meet a new criminal that lives here in town. We were let into Stan's house by Stan when we knocked on the door.

When I met Stan, I shook his hand and I introduced myself by telling him, "My name is Rick and I am a mafia man that mostly deals with the sale of potions."

Paul then told Stan, "This is the man that did away with your problem by making a hit on the eye witness in your court case."

Stan said, "Oh, well I am not sure if I wanted that done or not."

That is when Paul's face got beat red and he said angrily, "You better not be screwing me around or there is going to be hell to pay after what he did for you."

I was also getting to be upset with this man after he told us that. Then I remarked, "I was told by Paul if I took care of your problem you would pay me two hundred thousand dollars."

Stan mentioned, "Maybe I said something like that, but I didn't actually mean I wanted this done."

Paul yelled at the top of his lungs, "You said you wanted it done, no matter what!"

Stan then smarted back, "No I didn't!"

That's when I firmly stated, "Well you know what? You are going to pay me anyways, all two hundred thousand dollars' worth."

Stan sarcastically stammered, "No, I won't pay you. I don't have that kind of money!"

I raised my voice one more time and warned Stan, "You have a week to get my money. Yes, all of it or I'll make your life a living hell. Also," I explained to him "Don't think I can't come back and take you out for ripping me off. One more thing, don't you dare go to the law and be a dirty little rat. There are other mafia men out there that will dispose of you for me as a favor with no problems." That was the last time I said something to him.

Paul then snapped, "And one more thing from me, don't think this is a war you can win."

After that we left Stan's home, slammed the door, and drove back to Paul's place.

Chapter 3

It was Saturday afternoon, almost a week since the incident with Stan, and my wife asked if we could plant a garden in a greenhouse. She asked this question about planting a greenhouse two weeks ago. We don't own a greenhouse so today we are going downtown and we looking into buying a greenhouse. I had been thinking Mega Size Hardware might sell them, so we would stop there first.

"Let's get in the automobile with our children and drive downtown," Linda told me.

All four of us made our way to the garage and we decided to take Linda's automobile because my truck lacks a backseat. All three children squeezed into the back seat and I was going to drive for Linda. We both got inside the car with me behind the steering wheel and Linda in the passenger seat. I started the automobile, backed out of the garage, and then backed out of the driveway onto the street in the front of my house. I then started driving down to the hardware store in downtown Greens City. After a thirty-five minute drive, we pulled up into the hardware store's parking lot and I noticed the gardening supplies that were outdoors behind the store.

We entered the store and one of the cashiers said, "Welcome to Mega Size Hardware, what can I help you find?"

I answered with a question, "Do you sell greenhouses for planting a small garden?"

"If you walk all the way to the back of the store and go out the back door of the store you will find everything gardening. We have taken all of our gardening supplies to the back of the store now that it is changing into spring."

After we have walked out of the back of the store, my wife and I noticed three different sizes of greenhouses.

"The small one and the medium one are both too small," I said to my wife. "Let's just get the big one. It's not much more expensive than the other two," I discussed with my wife.

Linda remarked, "That one is probably big enough as well."

We paid for the greenhouse, tied it to the roof of our car, and drove home. When we were home with the greenhouse, I had the chore of unpacking it from its flat rectangular box and assembling it. I took out all the contents of the box and organized all of it in the back screened-in porch.

I told my wife, "I will actually finish building the greenhouse tomorrow." She replied with, "That would be just fine."

It was Sunday morning and my family was at a Catholic church which was the church they attended every week. My wife spent time every Sunday trying to make sure our children were always being good by the Catholic faith. I spend time with my religion on Sunday morning performing a Satanic ritual for myself by the *Man's Book of the Law*, LaVeyan Satanism. I always ended with the prayer, "Enter good and enter evil by the man and to his steeple pray to god and to his people. Pray to darkness and pray to light, that I may gain life's true sight. I am a man that's not too moral, so strike me down with good and evil, Amen."

When church ended for my wife and children, she came home to cook our tradition of a better and more expensive meal. We always have a better meal on Sunday at noon to celebrate the Sabbath. At that point, while my wife was going to cook, I put together her green house. The greenhouse came with directions, so I read those first and then began to assemble it. I worked for about an hour and a half on this somewhat difficult project/

I was only about half-way done when I heard my wife come out the back door to tell me, "Dinner time, if you want to take a break and come eat with your family."

Over dinner, my wife and I just talked about what kind of plants she wanted in her greenhouse. I was preoccupied thinking about going over to

Stan's house tonight and demanding the money I said he owes me. I gave him a week to have my money and now it's been a week. After dinner I finished building our new green house, which took me about another hour.

I then went back inside our house and told my wife, "It's done, so go look to see if it is to your liking or not."

She walked into the backyard, through the greenhouse door, and said, "It's perfect." Then she hugged and kissed me and went back inside to plan out the plants she wanted to grow.

It was seven o'clock in the evening on Sunday night and I was on my way to Stan the thief's house. As I pulled up into Stan's driveway I noticed Paul the Pimp was here as well. I had a pistol hiding under my jacket so he won't be able to screw around. As I walked up to the door, Paul opened it as I was about to knock and let me in. Stan was sitting on the sofa he owned in his living room and I took a seat on an easy chair across the room from him.

Stan immediately stammered, "I don't have your money yet. I only own about ten grand right now so just let it go that I owe you for this."

I said, "No, I want my money and I want it now!"

"Well I don't have it and I probably never will," he stated as he started to cry when I pointed my pistol at his chest.

I told him, "This is unacceptable" and then I said, "Goodbye." I pulled the trigger on my pistol and it went off with a *Bang!* I missed on propose to scare him into paying me. I told him, "You better get my money soon or the next one will be for good."

Paul interrupted and said to me, "I will pay you the money he owes you and then I will keep coming back to Stan's house to make him pay me one hundred dollars per week payments until he pays me back." Paul then added, "It's the least I can do since I am the one who told you about the job."

I responded with, "I am fine with that, if that's what you want to do."

Chapter 4

It was about two weeks of me selling small amounts of potion out of my basement after the whole Stan incident. However, most of my customers just weren't buying large amounts like usual. Robby, my potion cook, doesn't ever sell potion to people he doesn't know and only to people he believes he can trust.

I did have an interesting customer stop over at my house yesterday. It was on an early Saturday morning when he showed up to buy some of my noxious supplies. He claimed to be part of a traveling orchestra. He happened to be the orchestra conductor that had run into Robby and he wanted to buy some potion.

Robby apparently said, "No, I don't trust people I don't know but go to this address here and talk to Rick."

After I let the orchestra conductor into my house, he introduced himself with, "Hello, my name is John, John Anderson, and I am a traveling musician."

"It's nice to meet your acquaintance John. My name is Rick," I calmly introduced myself.

"What can I do for you today?" I questioned John.

He replied, "I want some potion and a lot of it because I have a whole orchestra that wants some of what you supposedly sell."

I told him, "It's two dollars per dose usually."

He then came back with, "So how much can I get for four hundred dollars?"

"I will sell you two hundred doses for that price," I answered. "I will charge one dollar per dose if you purchase one thousand or more," I told him the deal.

John then replied, "I don't have that kind of money on me, so just sell me the two hundred."

I added, "Did you bring something to put the potion in?"

John answered that question with, "In my automobile I have an empty cello case. Will that work?"

"Yes, an empty cello case will work, if you could walk out and get it," I told him.

John quickly walked back to his automobile, got the case, walked back in, and handed it to me.

"Let me run down to the basement, get what you want, and then I will come right back up," I said to the musician.

I quickly opened the vault in the floor, counted out two hundred doses, closed the cello case on them, and made my way back upstairs. I then took the payment from John, gave him the cello case, and then I said to John, "It should all be there."

John remarked, "Well, that was easier than I thought it would be. Thank you for your business and I will just let myself out."

I nodded goodbye and told him, "Have a nice rest of your day," as he was walking out the door.

Now, the point of this story is the fact that Robby didn't want to sell the musician anything because he didn't know or trust the musician. This is also true about the way I do business selling potions. I don't want to deal with people I don't know either and Robby opened his stupid mouth about my illegal activities. Now I must drive down to Robby's house and holler at him for telling someone I sell illegal potion. The only reason I sold the musician anything is because I could tell he wasn't lying so he probably was not an undercover officer for the brilliant Catholic government. It is not urgent to go tell Robby to never tell anyone about me ever again. Unless I decide to meet with someone and I am the one telling them I sell potion. I will just make sure I remember to talk to him next time I see him.

My best customer Jennifer Nicolson showed up. She had recently bought a large amount of potion and I would have thought she would still have quite a bit. Oh well, I was wrong and Jennifer didn't have any potion.

After Jennifer walked into my home she asked, "Do you still have any potion?"

I asked, "How much do you want?"

She then said, "How much can I just have?"

In a soft voice I asked, "It sounds like you want some for free?"

She remarked, "Well, I am a good customer and I don't have any money right now."

"There is no way I give anyone anything for free, especially potion," I stated in a firm voice. Knowing her profession, I should have realized she would try this one on me and it is not going to work.

In somewhat of a sexy voice she said, "Maybe, we could arrange another way to for me to pay you." She then put her hand up my shirt and started feeling my stomach.

I pulled her hand off me and I said, "No way is this going to happen between us for two reasons. First, I do business with expensive goods and losing money in a deal like this is something I never do," I explained. "Second, I maybe a criminal but I am a married man with a family that I do not want to lose." This was probably the real reason I don't want this to happen.

"Yeah, but I really need it right now," Jennifer said while she was starting to cry.

I still said, "No money then no potion."

She then started to beg, "I had a really bad night last night and I need you to do me this one favor. Please, can you?"

"I am in the business of selling potions," I told her, "Not handing out favors. So unless you are going to buy something you can just get out of here."

Then Jennifer screamed, "I don't know what your problem is Rick, just give me some potion so I can leave."

"I told you, no potions for free. So get out of my house if you are going to yell."

She yelled back, "I am not going anywhere without potion, just hand it over now and I will leave."

"I am going to get really mad at you if you keep this up, so just get out of my house now," I said seriously and then told her, "You can come back when you have some money but until you do, no potion."

Then she said, "No, give it to me now!"

I got fed up, grabbed her by the arms, and pushed her outside. After she was all the way out, I slammed the door shut and locked it. She then picked up a rock and threw it at the house. She missed the windows, which I was happy about. She then left, walking through my yard and swearing at me at the top of her lungs.

Oh, well at least she is out of my house for now. She will come back when she has the money. I have had her do this at my house before, but usually when she comes back with money she isn't holding a grudge. If you were a mafia man for only two weeks, you would see how many other sorts of criminals will try to rip you off or try to get something for free. This is a dangerous part of the job when bad people, which we all are, go bad on each other.

An hour later I heard an automobile pull up into my driveway. Then I heard the door slam hard so I looked outside and it was Paul the Pimp. He walked up to the front door of my house and banged on it about as hard as he could. I was not happy about him almost breaking my door down.

I answered the door and Paul said, "Could I come in and talk you?"

"Yes, fine, just come right in and find a place to sit." I asked the next question, "What is it that you exactly need from me Paul?"

"You were abusive to one of my fine ladies and it was Jennifer you were rough with," Paul said.

"Yeah, well, that is what is going to happen if she walks in to my house and starts yelling at me because she can't get what she wants for free," I firmly stated.

Paul commented, "I'm taking it that she wanted potions for free?"

"Yes," I answered. "I said no and she started yelling at me. I don't need to put up with that."

Paul asked, "Well, why did she say you were pushing her around?"

"I only pushed her once and that was out the front door," and I was telling him the truth. "She didn't get hurt at all from the whole deal anyways and that's because I wasn't being that violent."

"My problem with this one is I don't like it when men rough up my ladies," Paul said in a light tone. She didn't tell me the truth about what happened over here and she made it sound worse than it was," Paul then mentioned and then added, "If she is going to cause these types of problems like wanting something for nothing, I can't do anything about it and this is what she needs to understand."

"It's fine," I said to Paul. "I've had people do worse over here because of potion."

Paul added one remark before he left. He said, "I am going to talk to her about this one so she stops causing problems for people. Goodbye Rick, I am going to leave."

As Paul left I said, "Goodbye."

It was four-thirty in the afternoon on a Friday when I got a surprise visit from three teenagers. School had just ended for the weekend and they are looking for good times while they were still young. I knew two of the teens because I had sold them potion before. I could tell the third one was trying to prove himself a man in front of his peers by using potion. He seemed plenty nervous about this idea. They didn't buy potion very often because they never had any money, but when they did have some money they always spent it on potion.

I let these three into my house and they immediately said, "Can we buy some potion?"

I asked, "How much?"

They answered back, "How much can we get for ten dollars?"

I explained, "Five doses of potion for ten dollars."

Then one of them cut me off talking to each other. He said, "There is only the three of us so we only needed three doses which is six dollars. Then we have enough money to buy a pack of cigarettes for the night as well."

"That'll work," one of the other teenagers said. Then he said, "Give us three doses for six dollars."

I handed the three doses to the three teenagers and they then handed me their six dollars.

They said to the new kid, "We are doing this at your house tonight because your family is out of town and you have the house to yourself."

"We will wait until tonight at about eight o'clock and then we will start having some fun," one of the teenagers said.

Another one of these three teenagers said, "Next, we have to buy some cigarettes so where do we get some cigarettes?"

I asked them this last question to try to get them to leave, "Is the potion you bought satisfactory?"

"Yes," they said then they all decided. "Now we have to leave to find a place to buy cigarettes."

Then the new kid said, "Who do we know that has a pack of cigarettes for sale?"

One of them chirped up, "I know a few places to try, so let's leave and find this last thing we need for tonight.

All three of them said, "Goodbye Rick," and left out the front door.

There has always been one thing I do as a mafia man that has always bothered me. This terrible deed of mine bothers me to the point that I feel almost haunted with guilt. I over time I have made a lot of adult decisions possible for children. It never used to bother me but that was before I had kids of my own. Now I know I would never want my children to do these types of things especially before they had made decisions with what to do with their lives as adults. If they do things that they are not able to understand at a young age, then these things may be what they still do with the rest of their lives.

It doesn't happen much, but every now and then a very wealthy man or woman wants to spend a night or two around some potion. Lots of times it is someone that works for the Catholic government. This means they must find a way to get a hold of something that they keep illegally and who is stupid enough to sell potions to the government. I know it's true that the government knows I sell potion but they don't catch me. I got a visit from some government officials and they said, after I opened the front door, "We want to buy potion from you so we can have some adult fun time. We won't bust you for it this time."

After I heard this line I told them, "I don't know what you're talking about. I don't ever have any potion over here so you are wrong about me." Yes, this was a lie, but I am not selling potion to the government.

"Rick, it's fine tonight. We do know what you do so just sell us a little bit of potion." This is what they said to me and I didn't trust them at all.

I said, "I'm sorry you have it all wrong. There is nothing like that over here." I was starting to get a little nervous and so I told them flat out lies.

Then it happened, "Let's just go in anyways, find what we want, take it, and then leave."

Right then, I was realizing my vault in the basement was not hidden and locked.

The government then forced their way in. One of them said, "You go downstairs, I will take the main floor and you take the upstairs. As soon as they went into the basement they hollered upstairs and said, "I found it down here in the basement. I am just going to take about twenty doses." He then came upstairs with a small backpack that he came into my house with and asked, "How much do twenty doses cost?"

I said, "Forty dollars".

The man with the backpack pulled out his bill fold and placed two twenty dollar bills on the table.

"That's all we need, so let's get out of here and go have some dangerous fun," one of the government employees loudly spoke.

After that, the government officials walked out the door, closed it, got into their vehicle, and drove away. I was thinking that I could have sold them potions without being arrested, but what criminal actually trusts the law?

Chapter 5

For the most part, people who know me know that I make my money selling potion. As a professional mafia man, I can make a little dough doing other things which can be somewhat worse than what I usually do. I am a mafia man in large city known as Greens City but there are other cities for a decent mafia to work in. I could be considered one of the greatest mafia men of all time because I never get caught. There are jobs mafia men are hired to do, sometimes for other mafias.

I was in my wife's vehicle driving to Yarbrough City, a city that is about half the size of Greens City. I had received a letter in the mail from an organized crime syndicate called the Mixed Mafia. I borrowed her automobile because the truck is hard to drive on the highway this far. The letter promised at least three million dollars for some wet work, which meant this could get bloody.

The Mixed Mafia is a strange operation because they make their money in high–end, almost military, attempts to steal expensive objects. Sometimes this mafia may sell art, gold, jewels, and who knows what else. These are jobs this mafia can handle but for jobs that are a little more serious they use hired hands. With a big paycheck from this group, I can be coerced to do anything they want since I do whatever I want anyways.

After four and a half days of driving and staying in hotels overnight, I finally reached my destination. I pulled over into the first service station I saw so I could open my suitcase to find the address for the house I was supposed to be at. The address read, "4543 Cold Brook Road". I had also brought a map of Yarbrough City with me. I studied the map and decided on an easy route through town.

I pulled up to an old gothic-style red brick house with the right address from my letter. The sun was just starting to go down at about seven o'clock, so I could see lights on in the house's first floor. I parked my automobile in front of the house on the street, since the driveway was full of two automobiles parked side by side in front of a two-stall garage. As I exited my vehicle I could see someone watching me from the house's front window. I thought they were probably watching me because these men, who were supposed to be a mafia, don't know I decided to do these jobs for them. I had met this mafia only once in my life, therefore I don't know them very well and they don't know me either. I was about halfway between my automobile and the front door when, before I made it to the front door, it opened and a large man stepped outside.

I could tell the man who stepped outside didn't recognize me because of the way he said, "Who are you supposed to be?"

I answered, "My name is Rick, people who know me call me Rick 'The Slick Man' Thompson and I showed up here to do some jobs for the Mixed Mafia."

"Oh yeah, I remember sending you a letter about two weeks ago," the man who stepped outside replied. "We were willing to pay a lot of money for these favors we need someone to do for us," the heavy-set man exclaimed.

I walked up to him, shook his hand, we both said hello to each other.

He said, "Thanks for responding so quickly. We have some things that we can't do ourselves." He then walked me inside and I waited to bring my luggage in until I know where I was going to be sleeping tonight.

On that note, the other mafia man inside told me, "There is an empty bedroom down in the basement where you can stay while you are in town working for us."

I replied by saying, "Well then give me a minute to grab my bag from my automobile."

The mafia man who let me in said to his eleven-year-old son, "Go run outside and bring him his things."

I then handed off my keys to him and said, "Everything I need is in the trunk."

About two minutes later, he walked back in with both my suitcases. He was not quite strong enough to carry them with both his hands but he eventually got it done.

"My name is Teddy Brown," said the man that let me in his home. Teddy was rather large in size. He was almost seven feet tall and weighed around three hundred pounds I'd estimate. "This man is my younger brother 'Shooter Brown'," Teddy introduced me to him. Shooter was a rather thin man but also tall. "You also showed up just in time for dinner. My wife is cooking a home-made pizza pie," Teddy told me.

After dinner, we were sitting in Teddy's family room having cocktails of vodka and club soda.

Teddy told me, "I will be going to bed about three hours from now. This way I can get up to meet with the rest of my men. If you get up early enough," Teddy said, "You can come with me and they can give you the details of the jobs we have for you."

I remarked back to Teddy, "I would want to come with you so I can get these jobs done as fast as I can."

A few drinks and a few hours later, Teddy told us, "I am going to my bedroom for the night," and said to his wife named Carla, "Would you like to join me?"

She replied with, "Yes, I am starting to get a bit sleepy. Bedtime sounds like a good idea."

Teddy's brother, who probably shouldn't drive on the account of his alcohol consumption, decided to go home for the night and said, "Goodbye" to the room and left.

Who knows, maybe he is used to drinking and driving.

I then took myself to the basement of Teddy's home, climbed into bed, set the alarm clock by the bed to wake me up at six-thirty in the morning, and then let myself fall asleep.

In the morning I heard Teddy's wife awake in the kitchen about twenty minutes before my alarm clock went off. I decided to get up now and not wait for the alarm to go off. I then unzipped one of my suitcases and picked out an outfit to wear today. I now realized that I had forgotten to pack a bath towel to use after I shower. I decided to go upstairs, talk to Carla, and ask if she could supply me with a bath towel.

I asked Carla politely, "Do you have a bath towel I can use to dry off with after a shower, since I forgot to pack one?"

In a nice fashion she said, "Sure," and walked through her house to a small closet by the restroom, opened it, grabbed a normal-sized blue towel, closed the closet, and handed it to me. She pointed into the restroom by the closet and told me, "Here is the restroom that we have a shower in, use it whenever you want."

I turned to Carla and said, "Thank you for the towel and for letting me shower." I stepped into the restroom, locked the door, and turned the water on.

When I walked out of the restroom after I had showered, Teddy was awake in the front family room, drinking a cup of hot coffee.

Carla asked me, "Would you like some coffee to start your day with?"

"I would appreciate a cup of coffee to help me finish waking up," I answered.

Teddy then said, "I think it is my turn to shower." This was after he finished drinking his coffee. He got up and walked into his bedroom to find something to wear for the day then walked into the restroom and took his shower.

Teddy was now out of the shower and he came into the family room and sat down. He told me, "We are going to leave in about an hour to meet with my mafia. We do have a job late tonight and you are welcome to come along if you want. You can make a little money off this one if you do decide to come and don't mind the idea of stealing. This job we have to do tonight isn't one of the jobs we were going to pay you to do."

I asked the question, "What is the job you have tonight?"

Teddy answered, "There is a priceless diamond that is being shown at a large shopping center here in town and we know what bank they move it to at night. Our mafia has decided we are going to burgle the bank and steal the diamond tonight. We know there is a large amount of gold bars at the same bank that we will take as well. That is how you can make some money if you help."

We pulled up in front of Donny Jameson's house which is where the Mixed Mafia would be meeting at to discuss tonight's job. There were about ten other automobiles parked in front of Donny's house. We walked into

Donny's house after he invited us in and said, "Alright, it looks like everybody is here. Let's get started."

Since I didn't know how large or small this mafia is I asked, "Is this all the more men you have in this mafia?"

Teddy answered me with, "Well we have about fifteen men here but actually we are about four times this size. On a job like this we like to have as few men as we need, this keeps anyone from seeing us while we work. This way there is not such a big crowd. We usually draw straws to see who is going to be doing a job, after we decide how we will do something then we decide how many men we need."

"Who is this guy? If I don't know him, I don't like him. He could get us caught," said a mafia man named Richie.

Teddy explained to him, "His name is Rick and he mostly deals in potions for a living, but he is here to do some jobs for us. We sent him a letter in the mail to Greens City and he drove down here to deal with Michael's murder case for us."

"I remember the letter because I am the one who mostly wrote it. Don't think I didn't already know that, I could be testing him," Richie snapped. "As far as the job tonight goes, the new guy needs to know to only do what he is told and don't screw up," Richie told the room.

"Just do what we are doing and we will explain on the way," Teddy explained.

"We will make two stops tonight after it gets dark out, one at a house and then the bank," this is what Donny decided to tell me.

It was now midnight, dark enough to do our job, so one of the mafia men went out to his automobile and brought in a large-sized duffel bag. He opened it and started to empty its contents which were twenty masks so nobody saw our faces, twenty pairs of gloves, and about ten pistols.

Donny told the room, "Grab a mask, a set of gloves, and a pistol." He also made the comment, "If you are driving one of the getaway vehicles, you are not allowed to carry a hand gun. Besides, you stay in the vehicle no matter what so you don't need one."

"The point of this one," Teddy said, "has to do with the police. If we get pulled over then we don't want the police to see any of our firearms. It is best the driver doesn't have one. The police can search the driver anytime that they want but they need a search warrant to search the passenger. The government claims that driving is a privilege not a right, so the driver can be searched any time." Teddy said this and then told us why the police can't search the passenger, "It is because they are not using the privilege to drive, so a warrant has to be issued."

The mafia decided that it is time to leave and begin our heist. We piled three men in each of the automobiles. We drove about thirty minutes across town and pulled up in front of a yellow painted house. Right then, they told me how we are going to pull of this burgle attempt.

Teddy explained, "So you know we are after a diamond in a bank. This house is the home of the man that runs the bank. Lucky for us he lives alone so there is no one that can run to the law for help except for him." Teddy continued to explain, "What we are actually going to do here is Richie, who is in the vehicle in front of us, will go knock on his door. When the banker wakes up and answers the door, Richie will flash a gun and back him up into his home. Richie will tell the banker, 'Go get your keys to open the bank and the vault inside the bank that you run.' The banker will then be told, 'Yes, we are robbing your bank. So no funny stuff and you might live.'"

Richie exited the vehicle he was in, made his way to the front door, and banged on it until the banker answered. He forced the banker straight back at gun point and slammed the door shut. About five minutes later, Richie and the banker quietly walked through the front lawn and into the automobile Richie was previously in. The automobile took off driving towards the bank and then the other few vehicles started driving behind him. When the first of the automobiles pulled up to the front of the bank, Richie got out and kept the banker locked in the vehicle. He waited for all the other automobiles to park then he motioned with his hand for everyone to get out and come stand in front of the bank. After everyone was there, Richie opened the door to his vehicle, grabbed the banker by the arm, and pulled him out. He then dragged the banker up to the front door of the bank.

Richie then asked the banker, "Is there an alarm system on this bank to tip off the fuzz?"

The banker answered, "Yes, it has to be deactivated once we are inside with a secret number you punch in on a keypad."

"Now don't lie, just tell us what the code is and where the keypad is at or we will have an accident," said Richie.

"The code is six-five-seven-eight. If you look through the front door windows onto the wall to the left you can see it," the banker nervously told us that. He also said, "You have to turn off the alarm within thirty seconds of unlocking the door."

Richie next asked the banker, "Which key unlocks the front door?"

The banker just pointed at the right key. The key worked to unlock the door and Richie ran to the keypad and entered the number. He could tell it had worked with the beep it gave him.

We all walked into the bank, then the banker was told by Richie, "Open the bank vault."

The banker did just that and using the combination lock on the vault, he opened it. Most everything was locked up into private security boxes except for the gold bars on the floor. The mafia men started to place the gold into empty duffel bags they had brought in with them.

Donny asked the next question, "Which one of these security boxes has the priceless diamond in it, that is on display at the shopping center, Mr. Banker?"

"That would be box two-twenty," the banker answered.

"Open it," was the next thing Donny said.

The banker replied, "I can't open a security box that has been rented out because the only key is owned by the person who owns the box and they keep that with them."

Donny mentioned, "I have a crow bar in my trunk. Let me go get it and I will see if that works." He went out to his vehicle and returned with a crowbar along with a small hand-held sledgehammer. Donny said, "Teddy, go hold the crowbar in the side of the security box and I will use this sledgehammer to pound the crowbar into place."

After two strikes on the crowbar, Teddy pulled back and the box broke open. He slid out a small box and then set it on the table in the bank vault. We opened the box and there it was, a priceless diamond. The diamond was placed inside of a small jewelry box. Teddy then placed it into one of the bags with the gold bars.

Teddy next pulled a think brown rope out of his duffel bag and then told the banker, "Go sit on the office chair that is behind the teller's front desk."

The banker did what Teddy asked probably because he did not want more problems than he already had. Teddy proceeded to tie the banker to the chair he was told to sit on.

I asked, "Why are we tying him down?"

Teddy answered, "If we bring him home and just let him go, he can summon the police to that area of town he lives in. If we tie him down, someone will find him in the morning when the bank opens and we will be far away by the time the police find out that this bank was robbed."

After we had the banker tied down, Donny looked around the bank to make sure we didn't leave anything behind.

"Alright," Donny said, "Grab all of the duffel bags, be as quite as possible, and let's leave the bank."

Everyone did as Donny said, they picked up everything we brought in with us and then made our way back to the automobiles. Once we were back into the getaway vehicles, each one of the drivers started up their automobile and we drove back to Teddy's place. When we pulled up in front of Teddy's home, everyone rushed the duffel bags full of our loot into the house, hopefully without alerting the neighbors.

"Here we are," Donny said in an excited voice. "Now that we are all inside, weigh up the gold." Donny wanted this done because nobody knew how much gold would be for the taking in the bank. When they were done counting the gold, they found out that they owned about seventy-four pounds of it.

My next question to the mafia was, "How do you intend on making any money from everything we stole?"

"Well, if you would have waited until tomorrow then you would have found out by yourself," Shooter, who one of the mafia man, responded. "Since, you are asking, however, there is a high-end jeweler that makes the world's finest and most expensive jewelry. The jeweler lives about five hundred miles away but he knows to be here tomorrow morning because today is the day we were supposed to do this job for him. He will be here with a payment of five and a half million for the gold and the diamond."

"It works out pretty well with this jeweler because it's hard to get caught by the law for this one," Donny added. "That's because he has a real nice way of laundering the gold and the diamond. He will melt down the gold, cut the diamond, and turn it into jewelry," the way Donny told me this sounded excited. "The smart part of the plan on the jeweler's end is that once the gold and diamond has been turned into jewelry, no one will know where the gold and diamonds have disappeared to."

I was still in bed the next day when I heard a conversation taking place upstairs. That's when I decided I would wake up. As I pulled myself out of bed, I glanced at the alarm clock and saw it was about seven o'clock in the morning. I walked upstairs and the first thing I saw was a big pile of cash with a man I had never seen before.

I introduced myself to the man with the cash by saying, "Good morning, my name is Rick. What is your name?"

He also introduced himself with, "Good morning, I go by the name Curt."

Teddy then came walking into the room then he told me, "He is the jeweler we did last night's job for and he is now getting ready to leave."

One duffel bag at a time, the jeweler loaded the gold into the trunk of his automobile. When he had all the gold that belonged to him, along with the diamond, he shook everyone's hand and let himself out. The jeweler then started up his vehicle and drove away after the deal he had made with this mafia.

Chapter 6

Today for lunch, I was at a small diner inside of a truck stop. I was eating a chicken sandwich with Teddy. He wanted to explain the dirty job I came here for. The three million dollar job that was in the letter I received from the Mixed Mafia.

Teddy started explaining to me, "Our mafia recently had a problem with the law and there is something we want done about it for our friend David Caldwell. He was caught stealing automobiles and he was put in prison for twenty years. What happened was he had an entire warehouse of stolen automobiles and when the state police kicked the door in, he was caught red-handed," Teddy told me this while he grumbled a bit. "We want you to make two hits, one on the judge that sentenced him and one on the prosecuting attorney that convicted him. The judge's name is Judge Scott Williams, the attorney is named Theresa Anne." Then Teddy said the worst thing, "This is supposed to send a message to the governments finest that you can't screw with us, no matter who you are."

I returned with the comment, "I think I can get this one done for you, if I know their names and the addresses where they live."

Teddy opened a briefcase and handed me a yellow envelope. Then he said, "Everything you need should be right in here."

I made the next comment, "I will look at it later when we are no longer in public."

"That's fine with me," Teddy said. "Let's just finish lunch and get out of here."

When we finished our meal, we made our way out to Teddy's vehicle and drove back to his place. I had started looking at the information Teddy handed at the diner we had eaten at. I think I know how I will do to these legal figures in. Firstly I need clean handgun that cannot be traced back to me. I do not have any connections in this city so I went and asked Teddy about it.

Teddy said, "I know a small arms dealer in town. Why don't we make a drive to see him?" Teddy also told me, "The arms dealer kind of owes me for something right now. I don't think I will make him pay up but that will keep him from screwing around."

We drove over to Eric Mathew's place in the slum of the city. Eric is the arms dealer I intended on buying a small handgun from. When we were inside Eric's one-bedroom apartment he walked us back into a closet in his bedroom. When he opened the small closet, I saw quite a few nice choices of firearms hanging on the wall. There were also some smaller pistols that were in the top drawer of a dresser that he opened.

I pointed at a Barretta Model 1934 and asked, "How much for the small Barretta?"

He answered with, "That one is a little bit cheaper because it was used in a murder case that was never solved. With used weapons like that, we file down the serial numbers on the gun and then we can sell it again," Eric added.

I asked Eric, "If I am going to buy a gun that is on sale then what is the price?"

"This one, I will sell you the gun for fifty dollars."

I reached into my back pocket, pulled out my brown leather billfold, took out two twenty dollar bills and a ten-dollar bill and handed it to Eric. "I will take the used Barretta for fifty dollars," I told Eric. I then asked, "Do you have a way to keep it quiet?"

He answered with the question, "You mean a silencer?"

"Yes," I replied.

"Hold on, I have accessories under the bed," Eric said as he as he knelt to the ground. He then slid a large plastic bin out from underneath the bed. He opened it and pulled out a silencer that matched the gun and it screwed right onto the barrel of the gun.

After the sale, I asked Eric, "How much money do you make being an arms dealer?"

He answered with, "About twenty million dollars per year."

I was curious why he lived in a neighborhood that was poverty stricken, so I asked him, "Why do you live in less fortunate neighborhood if you make that kind of money?"

"To answer your question," Eric said, "It is easier to get away with selling illegal guns in a poor neighborhood like this one. The people here do not like the government much so if they see or notice anything like an illegal firearm, they probably won't go to the law about it."

Teddy asked me, "Are you satisfied with the sale on the handgun then?"

"Yes, I am happy with the sale," I replied to Teddy. "And I like the lower price on a used gun since I will only use it once."

"Well then, if its fine with you Rick, let's get out of here and go back to my place."

We climbed into Teddy's vehicle that we had driven here and then drove back to Teddy's place. In my head, I was trying to plot the two murders that I was going to commit tonight. I was having a hard time deciding what to do with their families that will be at their homes. I suppose I will just kill them all inside of their homes so there will be no witnesses. It is usually easy to get away with murder when you don't know the person you will be killing. The law will have a hard time connecting the dots if you don't have a motive by knowing the victim.

It was eleven o'clock in the evening and I was getting myself ready to complete the task I came here to do. First, I made sure they couldn't track my footprints so I put on a new pair of shoes. Then I put on two gloves so there would be no fingerprints left behind. I put my pistol that I had just purchased in a holster under my brown leather jacket. I then put on a rubber mask that looked like a normal person's face in the dark. This way no one could identify what I look like.

With a straightened-out paperclip and a small screwdriver, I created a way to pick the lock at my victim's house. I do have the skill to pick a lock, all you have to do is push down on all the pins inside the lock one at a time while a screwdriver is used to turn the lock. I think I will make one hit tonight on Judge Scott Williams and tomorrow I would take down the prosecutor Theresa Anna. I pulled out a map of Yarbrough City to decide on a route to Judge William's house. I needed a map in this city to show me the best way to get to Judge William's house because I don't live in this city. After deciding on a route to the judge's house, I walked out to my vehicle, got in, and proceeded to drive across town.

I found the judge's house in the dark at almost midnight and there were no lights on. I parked my automobile three blocks away and then walked the three blocks to his house. After I had made my way to his front door, I reached into my pocket, pulled the lockpick out of my pocket that I had made from a paperclip, and then I pulled out the screwdriver. I placed the paperclip inside the lock, spent about five minutes picking the lock, and I eventually forced the door to unlock.

After I had let myself into the house, I shut the door with as little sound as possible. I remembered from the paperwork that Teddy gave me that the judge's bedroom was on the main floor and his two children sleep on the second floor. As I walked through the front room, I saw a short hallway to my right. I noticed two bedrooms and a bathroom down the hall. I thought one of those bedrooms must be where the judge sleeps. I made my way down the hall then looked in one of the bedrooms. Sure enough there was the judge, fast asleep.

I next reached under my jacket, pulled the pistol out, and slowly made my way through the bedroom. When I was standing over the sleeping judge, I carefully aimed my handgun at his heart. I then pulled the trigger four times, two into the judge and two into his wife. One bullet went into the heart, one into the head in both my victims. The shots I fired were completely silent and I knew I wasn't going to assassinate the judge's whole family. Since his children were asleep and this didn't wake them up, I figured I would let them live. Besides they were innocent little kids. I took one look around and made sure I didn't touch anything or leave anything behind. I let myself out of Judge William's house and walked back to my vehicle three blocks away.

I then drove about twenty miles out of town until I found a dirt road with no one around. I burned the shoes, gloves, socks, jacket, mask, shirt, and pants

I had on during the crime I just committed. The only thing I kept was the gun, because I was going to use it tomorrow night when I killed the prosecutor.

When I got back to Teddy's, he was awake and asked me, "How did it go?"

I answered, "Everything went as planned with no problems."

Then I went to bed for the night after I said, "Good night, Teddy."

The next day, Donny showed up at Teddy's house and asked me, "How did it go last night with the job you did for us?"

I answered with, "I think it went well. The law shouldn't be able to pin anything on me. However, I am only half way done."

Donny asked with some surprise, "What do you mean half?"

"I only did the judge in last night but tonight I will kill the prosecutor," I answered.

"That's fine if that is the way you wanted to do it," Teddy remarked.

"I did it this way so I can concentrate on what I am doing on each hit." I told them that so they didn't think I was slacking or maybe think that I didn't want to do this job for them. However, neither one of them seemed to be upset about it.

That night I prepared the same way as I did the night before to take out the attorney for prosecuting David Caldwell. I would go through another new set of shoes and gloves to take out the trash. It was getting late, about time to drive over to the home of Theresa Anne's, and that is what I did. As I drove by her house, I noticed that her lights were on and everyone in her home was awake.

Well, that is fine, I thought, *I will just have to do this one a little bit different.*

I parked my car three blocks away like I had done the night before. The plan tonight was to walk up to the door and try the door handle to see if it is locked. I walked up to her front door to see if it is locked or not. I was lucky, it wasn't locked. I reached under my jacket, grabbed my handgun, and then ran into her house shooting. It only took about ten seconds to murder the entire house. My guess was the three dead children I blew away were hers and the man that was in the house was her husband. After I shot everybody dead with a silenced pistol, I looked around to make sure I didn't leave anything behind. I didn't see anything out of place, so I left and walked the three blocks back to my automobile. I got in my vehicle and drove out of town to the same dirt road I was at the night before. I burned everything I had with me again, although this time I had driven further down the road to a small river that I knew was out here. I then wiped any possible fingerprints off the gun with some rubbing alcohol that I brought with me for this purpose. After I had cleaned the handgun, I threw it into the river to get rid of all the evidence.

I drove back into town to Teddy's place. When I got there, everyone was sleeping. I also decided to make my way to bed and when I did that, I fell asleep after setting the alarm clock that sits on the small table by my bed.

I woke in the morning knowing I must get paid for the hits I made. After I get the money the Mixed Mafia owes me, I will get back on the road and drive home.

The first thing I said to anyone after my shower was, "I need to be paid my three million dollars I was promised. I want it today if possible. This way I can get on the road and get home," I said to Teddy.

Teddy decided that he could do this today and said, "If you can wait for me to shower, we can go to my bank and I will withdraw the money."

"That is fine," I said back to Teddy. "I will just sit here and wait."

Teddy put down the coffee he was drinking then said, "I will hurry up and take a quick shower."

I replied, "Take your time in getting ready, it isn't that important."

Teddy walked out of the restroom with clean clothes on for the day and he was still drying his hair with a towel. He then walked into his bedrooms and, somewhat talking to himself, I heard him say, "Where are my automobile keys?" I heard a jingle from Teddy's room and then Teddy said, "There they are" and it sounded like he dropped them into his pocket. He walked back into the restroom, put the damp towel back onto its hook, combed his hair into a part and hair-sprayed it into place. Teddy walked up to me in the front family room of his house and said, "Are you ready to drive to the bank and get your pay?"

I answered with "Yes and would it be possible to drive my automobile? This way I can put the money straight into the trunk instead of taking it from your vehicle and then transferring it to mine when we get back here to your house."

Teddy answered back with, "That would be fine and I will take my vehicle, so you don't have to drive me back here after we leave the bank."

"Good," I replied to Teddy, "Then I can get straight on the road instead of having to bring you back home."

Donny decided to ride down to the bank with Teddy while I followed them in my automobile. We pulled into the parking lot of a bank that was named Bank of United Trusts. Then Teddy and Donny exited their vehicle while I exited mine.

We walked through the front glass windows of the bank and to the bank teller.

Teddy told the bank teller, "I need to make a withdrawal and a rather large one."

The teller asked, "How big of a withdrawal do you plan on making from our bank?"

"I want to withdraw three million dollars and then have it placed into the trunk of Rick's automobile."

"I will have to let you speak to our bank manager for a transaction this size." The teller then said, "Follow me over to the manager's office in the corner of the bank."

When we walked into the banker's office, he greeted us with, "Hello and what can I do for you?"

"I want to withdraw three million dollars," Teddy said.

Then we got some bad news from the bank manager because he told us, "We must wait twenty-four hours to have this much cash because our bank isn't big enough to always hold that much. Give me a minute to look at your account and if the money is there then I will make a request from our main branch office to have this much money here tomorrow," the banker explained. The banker then asked, "I will be right back from checking your account to see if you have those kind of funds. What is your name?"

"My name is Teddy Brown," he told the bank manager as he walked away from us.

About five minutes later, the bank manager returned. He had good news which he explained to Teddy, "You do have the funds but I need your signature on this contract. It claims you do intended on returning for the money in no longer than forty-eight hours."

Teddy signed the contract, then he turned to me and said, "I guess you will be in town for one more night."

We left the bank and I was somewhat unhappy that I must wait in town until tomorrow. After this incident, we made our way back to Teddy's place for another night.

After Teddy, Donny, and I were awake and ready the next day, we made our way back to the bank. Like we planned yesterday, I took my vehicle to the bank and Teddy took his. This way I could leave town from the bank after being paid and Teddy could drive back home. For the second time, we walked through the front glass doors of the bank and then walked up to the teller at the front of the bank. It happened to be the same teller as yesterday.

She must have remembered us because she said, "Hi Teddy, are you back for your large withdrawal?"

"I happen to be here for that exact reason," Teddy answered.

The bank manager must have heard us talking to the teller because he hollered, "Bring them back here to my office!"

The teller did just that, she started to walk over to the banker then motioned for us to follow her and said to us, "Follow me."

We entered the banker's office and he acknowledged us, "How are you gentlemen today?"

Teddy is the only one that answered, "I am doing fine today. Were you able to get the money for the large withdrawal I want to make today?"

The banker responded with, "Absolutely, I have it locked inside the bank vault so just follow me and we will get you what you want."

We followed him to the bank vault and he unlocked the door to the vault after inputting the combination to the door. When the door to the vault opened, the banker said, "All the money on the floor in the burlap sacks are the three million dollars you wanted to withdraw."

Donny asked the banker, "Can we start loading it into the trunk of Rick's automobile?"

The banker replied with, "Right after Teddy signs the transaction ticket that I have on this clipboard I am holding." Teddy signed the paperwork and then the bank manager said, "Okay, the money is all yours and you can keep the burlap sacks for free."

We immediately started to load all the cash into the trunk of my vehicle. After we had all the dough loaded into my vehicle, we said "Goodbye and thank you," to the banker.

We then shook each other's hands, mafia man to mafia man, and said, "Goodbye," to each other.

Now that I had been paid, I took off out of town and pointed my way back to Greens City.

Chapter 7

After returning to Greens City, the first thing I did was go home to see my wife and kids. As I walked inside my home I saw that my wife was there.

She greeted me with a hug and asked me, "How was your trip out of town?"

I answered with, "Everything went about as well as I could have hoped and I have three million dollars in the trunk of your automobile that I borrowed for the trip." I asked the same question back "How was your week while I was away?"

My wife told me, "My week was fine but Robby stopped over saying there is a problem with the law and wants you to go see him as soon as possible."

"If there is that big of a problem with Robby, I will wait until tomorrow to go see him so I can spend tonight relaxing after all the driving I did," I told my wife. I also added, "I think I am going to spend the night here with you and this bottle of scotch I bought on my way home. Would you like to have a glass?"

My wife said, "Yes, I would like a glass to calm down with."

I woke up in the morning a little hungover from the scotch the night before then I immediately remembered I must make a visit to see Robby and then find out what his problem is. To cure the hangover I was feeling, I walked into the restroom, opened our medicine cabinet, grabbed a bottle of aspirin that I opened and took out four small white pills that I swallowed.

I then proceeded to make a strong pot of coffee that I decided to let brew while I was in the shower. I finished off one full pot of coffee while I was reading the newspaper at my kitchen table. I made my way to my truck, started it up, I backed out on to the street, and drove to Robby's house.

When I knocked on Robby's front door it took him almost two minutes to answer. He eventually answered and said, "You scared me. I thought you might be one of the police officer's that keeps driving by my house."

I asked Robby, who was a paranoid mess, "Can I come in?"

"Yeah, come right on in and then maybe you can tell me what to do about this mess I am in."

After I walked into Robby's house I asked, "What kind of mess are you in?"

"Well as you already know, I cook potion that I sell to various customers which includes you as my best customer," Robby told me. "Part of cooking potion is I need to find hard ingredients. I can get them from three different sources." Robby continued, "All three sources import the goods from other places on cargo ships. They never have had any problems until the last shipment got busted," Robby went on. "One of the importers had been busted because someone on the inside decided to be a little snitch. The government forced their way inside his shipping container on the ship when it landed. They found illegal equipment and supplies. I received a visit from the importer's wife because she was told he is in jail. So she went to see him during visitation hours," Robby said.

"The importer told his wife, 'I was caught importing illegal materials',," Robby explained. "I went to visit him in jail and he told me not to trust anyone anymore because of a mafia spoiled brat that snitched on us," Robby said with an angry tone.

My next question was, "What is the name of the importer that has been busted?"

Robby spoke and answered my question with one name which was, "Timothy Draft."

I asked Robby, "Do we know the name of the man who snitched?"

Robby said, "Yes, it was in the paperwork that Timothy was given while he sat in jail."

I then asked, "Well then, who was it that decided to be a dirty rat?"

"Torture Taylor Tomgreskey is the man who snitched, along with the ten-man team he operates with," Robby said.

"Taylor has always been the worst mafia man ever for doing bad things that are only for fun," I exclaimed to Robby. "Everyone who knows him, calls him by his nickname Torture instead of Taylor, even his own mother calls him this," I said with a chuckle. "This nickname comes from what he likes to do to a man," I also said to Robby.

"He will even invent torture devices to use on someone, I guess to keep it interesting," Robby added.

The reason Taylor can do whatever he wants is because of who his father is and the fact that he is far worse. There is an interesting story on who Taylor Tomgreskey's father is. His father is known as the Godfather and he alone runs all mafias. If you have a mafia somewhere on this entire planet, then your mafia is being run by the Godfather no matter what. Someone might ask, "Why do they let him?" Well because all mafias make it that way for all mafias. The Godfather knows how to be the most organized criminal of all but he only organizes and administers for all mafias. The thing about someone who was chosen to be the Godfather is that he rarely breaks the law unless he absolutely must. What is the Godfather's real job? It is to represent all mafias, which is why he doesn't break the law. So we can have a front and center man.

"Since someone was busted, we need to make sure no one else has to go down that path," I remarked to Robby. I also asked, "What do you have here to get busted with?"

Robby answered, "Just my lab that I produce potions with."

"Let's load it in to your vehicle that you have parked in your garage," I told Robby. Then I added, "I have a place to put it for now, at least, while the heat is still on."

Robby asked, "Where are we going to bring everything?"

I answered with, "I have a storage garage across town that I own with a second identity. The government does not know that I have a second ID and hopefully they won't find out. Pop the trunk to your automobile so we can put all your lab equipment into it."

"That will take us five trips and about twenty minutes to get my lab to hide in the trunk of my small red convertible," Robby explained. "Look over there, it's a police officer parked around the corner and it looks like he is watching us," Robby said, looking out his living room window.

I told Robby, "Well, as long as we don't break the law in front of him while we drive by, hopefully he won't be able to pull us over and search your automobile."

"Okay, I will try to drive a little bit slower and pay attention to the street signs, so I don't accidently break a traffic law," Robby slowly spoke.

We opened the garage door and backed straight out onto Robby's driveway. After we backed onto the driveway, we saw the police officer parked about one block away around the corner. We could just barely see into his vehicle, enough to make out a pair of binoculars that were pointed right at us. I think this means Robby has been told on as well and we need to be careful when we are driving around town.

After we were done here, I am going to make some home visits, just so everybody in the crime business knows the police will be trying to bust us more than what is normal. I am also going to take all my illegal possessions to my garage as well, just in case the police kick my door in.

We backed onto the street and drove by the police officer, we hoped that he would stay where he is and not bother us. Right then the worst thing happened, the police officer started to follow us.

"Alright, now we have the law tailing us. We need to figure out what we need to do about it," Robby shrieked.

"Well, what we can't do is drive to the storage garage, because the police officer will follow us there and I won't have a secret ID or storage garage anymore," I said to Robby.

Robby asked, "Who do we know that the lives closest to where we are at right now?"

"No one," I told Robby. Then I said, "You live in an unfortunate neighborhood, so there is nowhere to go that is close to your place."

Robby remarked, "Yeah, you are right. It really doesn't matter were we go, everywhere we can go is the same amount of time."

"Okay Robby, we will drive to my house, without getting arrested I hope," I decided to tell him. "When the heat is off my place, then we make our way to the storage garage to get rid of your equipment," I told Robby.

On our way to my house we turned two times and when we made the second turn the cop didn't turn after us. I could tell Robby relaxed after the police decided not to follow us. Unfortunately, about three blocks later, another officer turned after us and now he was following close behind. Once again, Robby gripped the wheel and started to drive as cautiously as he could. Robby knew where I lived and he decided he would take the freeway though town. This freeway went almost directly to my home and when we turned onto it the police followed. After about fifteen minutes of driving on the freeway, we took a right onto an off ramp. This was the right exit to go to my home. We still hadn't been pulled over and when we took this turn the police did not follow. Once again, Robby relaxed and we thought we were home free. Well, we thought so until we were pulling into my driveway and there was another police officer parked about two blocks away from my street. We pulled into my driveway, turned off the vehicle, and then we went inside, knowing we are safe for now.

Robby asked me a question, "Now that we are inside, how do get rid of the law so I can ditch my equipment?"

"I suppose we need to come up with a plan that makes it safe to drive to the storage garage," I contemplated and told Robby.

"The hard part is getting to the garage and dropping off everything in my trunk," Robby said, deeply in thought.

"Once we get everything dropped off, I can safely drive home because there won't be anything illegal in the vehicle," Robby added.

"I am thinking of an idea that could work," I said to Robby.

Robby asked, "What is your brilliant idea if I might ask?"

"What we will do is stay at my place tonight. I will have a place for you to sleep," I instructed Robby. "We will wake up at four o'clock in the morning and there might not be a lawman watching my house that late. If there isn't a policeman watching us, we can drive straight to the garage and hide your supplies."

The alarm went off at precisely four o'clock in the morning and without turning on the lights to alert the fuzz, I made my way wake up Robby. He was sleeping in a spare bedroom at the top of the stairs on the second floor.

When I woke Robby up, I told him, "Keep the lights off and get dressed."

Robby must have forgotten what the plan was because he was not easy to wake up this early in the morning.

"Robby, wake up," I told him a second time. "It is time to bring your supplies to my storage garage. This way we don't get caught with illegal goods."

When he heard me say this, he woke right up and, in the dark, took off the pajamas I had lent him for the night and he put his clothes on from yesterday.

After we woke up, we looked out the window and we did not see any more police. We were in Robby's automobile driving to the storage garage to hide his equipment that is mostly illegal. We were hoping to get lucky enough not to run into any local law enforcement that was out this late. This idea to drive to the storage garage of mine this late keeps the police from watching us leave, but it will not keep us from getting pulled over on our trip.

"So far, we have not seen any law enforcement," I said to Robby, "Which is good for us because we are only two blocks away." I mentioned, "I can see the sign for the garage I rent." Then I asked Robby, "Do you see the sign that says Rent All Storage?"

"Yes, I can see the sign for the garage you rent," Robby answered.

Then I told Robby, "Take a right into the parking lot and…WAIT! There is a policeman right there coming right at us."

"How about we just circle the block and maybe he will just keep on going?" Robby asked.

"That's not a bad idea but instead of circling one block, try to circle three to lose the tail," I answered back to Robby. "Take a right at the next intersection, go three blocks, take another right, and then we should be able to turn back onto this street and right into the storage garages."

Robby turned right to lose the tail and luckily enough the officer just kept right on going straight. We drove around three blocks and then into the parking lot of the storage garage. We then drove to the end of the parking lot and down to the isle of storage garages to get to the garage I own. I opened the garage with a key that I had brought with me and pushed the garage open. I didn't have much in here besides some furniture and antique dishes to cook with.

We unloaded the trunk with Robby's things and then we drove back to my place. I decided I would do the same with the potions I had in the basement of my house but I will wait until the same time tomorrow. I normally wouldn't have helped a fellow criminal out like this but without Robby I could not easily procure potion.

I asked Robby, "Have you seen any more of our types to warn them that somebody is being a snitch?"

He answered, "No, I hadn't thought about that yet."

I remarked, "Well, maybe someone should do that so no one else gets busted."

I waited all day to bring my potion supply to my garage at four o'clock in the morning. I loaded up the back of my truck with all of my potion and then stretched a black tarp over it so no one could see what I was transporting. I brought it to my garage, opened the garage, unloaded my potion, and then drove back home. This time I did not see any police on my way to or from the garage I rent. This meant I would not be able to sell anything to make money and I will have to tell my customers I don't have anything for them. My customers will not appreciate this one, but it's better than getting caught.

Now that I was somewhat safe from the law, I was going to spend the day talking to other mafia men and gangsters. I wanted to make sure that they know that there is a rat and who it is so no one else gets busted. I am going to tell them that it was Timothy Draft that had gotten busted and how they got busted. He got busted by a snitch that happens to be the Godfather's son and he goes by the name Torture Taylor. My first stop in town to make sure no one else will be busted was to go and see Paul the Pimp. I decided on him since I know him better than some other criminals in town and he usually knows what's happening on the streets better than anybody else.

Paul let me in his house after I had knocked and he had a few of his beautiful working girls at his place. Paul asked me, "Do you want one on the house from McKenzie over there?"

She said, "No way does he get me for free."

Paul yelled at her saying, "You will do as I say or I will smack you all over the house."

I answered Paul with, "No, I don't think I need that because I am a happily married man with a family to think about." I started to talk to Paul about the police making a sizable bust by asking him, "Did you hear about Timothy Draft being caught by the law?"

"Yeah, I suppose I did hear about this and so did every other gangster in town," Paul answered.

"That is the kind of news I would have wanted to hear from you," I said to Paul. "I was out of town when it happened and since I have been back, I heard about this and I wanted to make sure everyone knew what happened. I was going to spend the day telling everybody this because I just wanted everybody to know what happened. That way no one else is busted," I said to Paul. "How did everyone find out about this?"

Paul answered, "Timothy paid his lawyer to tell everyone he knows in town with what happened. They are threatening twenty-five to fifty years prison time for Timothy."

"Well then, as long as everybody knows what happened, I don't need to spend today making sure no one else gets caught. Has anybody decided what to do with the Godfather's son that has runamuck on us?"

Paul told me, "I haven't heard anyone talking about what to do about it."

"Why did Taylor decide to start telling on everybody when he gets worse than anyone?"

"Apparently, he was busted on having illegal potions and the government was willing to cut him a deal if he became a police informant."

I asked Paul, "Does the Godfather know what happened here with his son?"

"He did hear about it right after it happened, but until he arrives here in Greens City he only knows his son was caught breaking the law," Paul informed me. "I don't think the Godfather knows his son snitched on everybody and I don't know if that will upset his father or not. So when the Godfather gets into town here, we will tell his father what he did and let him sort things out with his son," Paul noted.

I asked Paul, "Are you telling me that the Godfather is on his way into town?"

Paul replied with the answer, "Yes or at least that is what I heard. It was a few days later, on Saturday, that I received a visit from Robby and he told me, 'The Godfather would be at his son's condo in about two hours.'"

A mafia man was sent to tell the local criminals, that they would be allowed at his son's home if we wanted to be there for whatever his son had done in town. There is also a mafia man with the Godfather's son allowing us to be there and wait for the Godfather. The Godfather will be at his son's home after they are done having lunch at a local restaurant. This gives his son a chance to be a little worried about being a rat on everyone in town and it gives us time to get there. Robby and I waited about an hour at my place and then we made our way to the condo that Taylor owns here in town.

We walked into Taylor's home and I said, "Hello" to the mafia man that works under the Godfather.

He said, "Hello" to me and then introduced himself by saying, "I am the Don and my name is Charlie Banswood."

I introduce myself with, "My name is Rick. This is a co-worker of mine and his name is Robby."

The Don told both of us, "The Godfather will be here in about twenty minutes." He also mentioned, "It will be three o'clock sharp when the God-father will arrive."

It was three o'clock. There was a knock at the door and then it opened before anyone could open it. A big round man about six and a half feet tall walked in. He nodded to the Don and said, "Hello Gentlemen, I am the God-father and my name is Henry Tomgreskey."

There were criminals standing all over the room andwe all showed up to make sure the Godfather's son was made completely miserable and sorry for being a rat.

The Godfather grabbed a hold of a small chair, moved it directly in front of his son, and then he sat down on it.

"Taylor, you are my son," the Godfather spoke and then he added, "I un-derstand you have problems with the law. I hear you were caught with unlawful potions and this is fine, I don't care about that," the Godfather said to his son. "However, you chose to be in the mafia, as I did when I was young, and that was fine. I don't care about that either. Since you decided to be an organized criminal, there are certain things you were taught, things you have to do and things you are never allowed to do," The Godfather told him. The Godfather then asked, "I have heard you told on a potion importer, is this true?"

Taylor did answer with the truth and said "Yes, I did that, but it wasn't my fault."

The Godfather next asked, "Whose fault is it then?"

"The police made me do it," Taylor exclaimed.

"What I heard is that you snitched to get out of trouble with the law for the potion charge they put on you," the Godfather said to his son. "Now is this the truth or not?"

"I suppose it is the truth. You are right, that is what happened," Taylor explained to his father.

His father said back, "So this man whom you told on had been busted by you and the police, because of this I am now hearing that this man has lost the rest of his life, isn't that right?"

"Yes, I suppose this is true," Taylor answered.

"Since you caused a man to lose the rest of his life, you have to lose the rest of yours," the Godfather explained to his son.

Then suddenly, we heard a *BANG!* and the Godfather had pulled a pistol from under his sports jacket and had shot his son in the heart. Taylor had a seizure for about five minutes and then completely passed away in front of us.

The Godfather said to himself, "I am sorry I had to do this and to my own son, but I wouldn't allow this out of any mafia man, not without death anyways." Then the Godfather told the Don, "Clean all of this up and get rid of the body. This way no one has to see any of this, especially his mother."

Chapter 8

"The Godfather always had a way of making money through Paul the Pimp," I was explaining to my wife. "This is why the Godfather liked the dingy animal in the first place. Paul was always the most notorious man for treating women badly, I can testify to this myself. Watching him beat them senseless over fifty dollars that they had lost the night before had always bothered me and I don't quite know why. I had been part of prostitution rings with Paul a couple of times. It can be more disturbing than women having physical relations over money."

My wife asked, "Why can it seem so terrible to see women do this for a man even if its over money?"

"The main reason is because of what Paul told me that he has locked in his basement right now. That is, young boys and girls that will be sold permanently," I answered my wife.

Then my wife asked, "So then whoever has enough money to buy a child slave permanently, for who knows what reason, can talk to Paul and he can find what you want?"

"Even though I am a mafia man myself and I am not innocent either," I continued to ramble on, "I do think using children for this is as low as you can be as a criminal," which is what I really believed and so this is what I told my wife. "These six children that have been kidnapped are up for sale at an auction. This auction is going on this weekend on Saturday night at ten o'clock here in town." I told my wife this because I might attend.

My wife asked, "If this is going to bother you then why are you going?"

"Mostly I might attend because I was invited and not because I want to bid on these children as someone's property," I answered her. "They also want a decent mafia man to attend so I can help them get away with it. Paul is willing to pay me twenty grand to be there so they don't screw up and alert the law. This is why I think I will show up on Saturday night. Only to get paid a few grand and not because I care about what it is they are doing." I said this as I was only thinking I might attend and I was still not positive about it.

It was Saturday afternoon and I was at home answering the door to my usual customers that like to buy potion. I was turning away everyone who came to me for the products I supply them with. It was because of the recent increase in police activity with the bust of Timothy Draft that I was not agreeing to make any sales. I was also telling my customers that I don't even have any potion right now which was a flat out lie because I have all kinds of it in my storage garage. I was telling all my normal buyers that it is just too bad. I am not selling anything right now and some of them can be a huge pain in the neck over the potion I sell.

At about eight-thirty I heard a knock at the door and so I made my way across my home to answer it. When I answered the door, I saw Paul the Pimp standing in front of me. I nodded to Paul as I was letting him inside and out of the small thunderstorm we are currently having.

"Hello Paul, what can I do for you tonight?" I asked, knowing that he was here about his auction going on at his place tonight.

Paul answered my hello with a hello of his own. He then proceeded to ask me, "Are you planning on being at my place tonight for the business I am doing?"

"Yes, I was planning to leave my house at about nine-thirty and arrive at your place a little before ten o'clock," I answered him.

Paul asked the question, "Would you be able to come to my place a little early so I know if I can trust the men that will be there?" Paul then added, "I have never met these men and you are a better judge of character than I am, plus you make a decent lie detector. I just want you to make sure they are not the law before I let them into my home and have the auction we are selling children at. These men that will be there tonight are not the usual mafia scum that we are used to," Paul seemed a little nervous when he told me this.

I asked him, "Well then, where else do men like this come from if they are people who don't mind breaking the law?"

"These men are very wealthy, white-collar business men and they wanted for me to find them a young friend," Paul replied.

I asked, "How many children are for sale and how many businessmen will be there be making bids?"

"There will be six children for sale and about twenty-five business men that I will have at my home in the basement this evening," Paul answered.

"If that is what you need, I can be ready anytime you want," I explained to Paul.

"Let's go right now, I will give you a ride in my automobile to my house and then I can give you a ride back," Paul said.

"That would be fine Paul," I told him and then said, "Let me put some shoes on and I will be right out to your vehicle."

Now that we were back at Paul's house, we had about half an hour before the business men showed up. In Paul's basement he had six folding coffee tables set up with four chairs set up at each table. He also had a small assortment of different types of liquor set up on each table and a small keg of beer. With plenty of alcohol down here in Paul's basement, I decided that I would some-what enjoy my time here tonight. On that note, I decided to pour myself a whiskey on the rocks into a small cocktail glass and then I took a seat at one of the tables. The business men started to walk into Paul's home upstairs over the next fifteen minutes.

As they made their way into the basement, I said, "Hello," and I was at-tempting to read them one at a time to make sure they weren't acting funny. "If any of you are the law and we get busted, there will be hell to pay. I will in-troduce myself as a mafia man named Rick and I will kill you at home if any-thing goes south here tonight. You have met Paul, our neighborhood pimp, but you haven't met me a professional criminal and you don't want to cross me or everybody dies," I warned.

"When everybody is here that has been invited," Paul said, "I will bring out the merchandise." Paul entered the room after everyone that is supposed to be here had shown themselves. Paul then said, "I think everybody is here, so let's get started with the bidding."

Paul opened a door to a small bedroom in the basement and walked out six children that were all chained together. Three of the children were male and three were female. They were told by Paul, "Sit on the six chairs that are against the wall. The ones that do not have coffee tables in front of them."

One of the business men introduced himself as Mathew and asked, "Can we see what we will be buying a little better?"

Paul answered his question with a question of his own, "What do you mean see them better?"

"I mean with less clothes on. In fact with no clothes on," Mathew stated.

Paul replied with, "Yes, if everyone else is fine with that?"

All the business replied to Paul with a "yes" nod.

Paul took a set of keys out of his front pocket and proceeded to take the chains off all the children that were for sale. After he did that, he took all the children's clothes off as well. They were then made to sit back down on the chairs that they had already sat on.

Paul said to the first child that was to be auctioned off, "Stand up, spin in a circle two times, say your name, and then state your age".

The first child was a boy, he spun around two times. "My name is Jason and my age is eight years old," he said this while crying a little.

"The first bid on Jason is thirty thousand dollars and this is the minimum bid allowed on Jason," Paul said loudly.

The first bid was made at thirty-five thousand dollars and this is how it went for about forty-five minutes until all the children were paid for. All the business men that made a purchase walked their investments out into their automobiles and left Paul's place.

The rest of the businessmen went home empty-handed and one of them mentioned to Paul, "If you are going to do this again, let me know and I can try again to see if there is something I can afford next time."

After everyone was gone from Paul's house, he was going to have to give me a ride home, since he is the man who drove me here. We both talked about it and I had decided to spend the night at Paul's place because we had too much to drink.

In the morning, when Paul and I were awake, he drove me home. When I got home, I took a shower and put some clean clothes on. After that I was thinking about whatever I must do today. I couldn't think of anything so I guessed I would sit at home and listen to the radio.

A few days after the auction, when it was about three thirty in the afternoon, I had a dark and terrible visit from the Godfather. He knocked on my door and I answered it. The Godfather walked in and he was just furious. The Godfather was armed with two pistols and two other mafia men who were with him also had two pistols. It sure seemed like the Godfather had a bone to pick with me and I couldn't think of a reason why.

He walked through my home and told the other two men that were with him, "Sit down on his sofa." Then he took a seat on my recliner while he pointed at a chair he told me, "Have a seat across from me on that chair." The Godfather started by saying, "You really caused Paul the Pimp and I a huge problem."

I asked, "What are you talking about?"

The Godfather answered by saying, "A few nights ago you attended an auction at Paul's place, is this correct?"

"This is correct, he was auctioning off some small children in his basement and wanted me to be there to help him get away with it," I told him.

"Well, it looks like you did the exact opposite and got everybody at the party busted," The Godfather explained.

"Yeah well, I don't think that is true. I didn't snitch on anyone, so I don't think that is probably what happened," I said in an aggravated fashion.

The Godfather, reaching into his suit pocked, grabbed a small tape recorder and said, "Yeah well, listen to this, even though you didn't do this on purpose."

He pushed play on the tape recorder and I started listening to a conversation that was between my wife Linda and me. We listened for a little over a minute and then I did recognize this conversation. This was the conversation I had with my wife the morning of the auction at Paul's home.

I had to ask the question, "Where did this recording come from? My wife and I didn't record any of this."

"Paul gave me a copy of this recording from jail. Then he told me that the fuzz has your placed bugged," the Godfather said.

"That night after the auction, all the business men were pulled over in their vehicles," he explained. "Every one of the businessmen with one of the children in their automobiles was arrested," he said with angry tones. "All the men that were arrested cut a deal with the law, by telling on Paul and that is who I am unhappy with right now," he said.

"Since you were the one who slipped up, even though it was an accident, I want you to deal with it," the Godfather stated.

I then asked, "What do you want me to do about it?"

He answered and said, "Kill all six of those rats, make it messy, and do it for Paul."

"Fine, I will get it done. They are as good as dead for telling on Paul," I said to the Godfather. "I do have one question. Can you supply me with two men that I can work with?"

"It is as good as done," the Godfather said to me and then he asked, "When do you want them?"

I answered the Godfather with, "Two weeks from now on Saturday afternoon. I want them at my place in the afternoon. This way we can plan out what I want done that night."

It was two weeks later, we were going to get revenge for Paul and on the businessmen that snitched on him. I had two men at my place that the Godfather had appointed. These men were going to help me kill the businessmen that told on Paul for selling child prostitutes. What we had set up to get them dead was supposed to trick the law. The two mafia men that were going to help me kill the six businessmen were named Travis and Luke.

"Let's get started Travis and Luke. I have a plan to get rid of the businessmen that told on Paul," I told the two mafia men. "What I want is for us to round up all six of these men at a house owned by one of these men," I explained. "First, I want us to have a home picked out to round them up at," I explained. "Then I want one of you to guard these men at the house we pick out while we escort all of these men to the same house by force," I exclaimed in an unpleasant voice. "I will tell you gentlemen what we are going to do next after everyone is at the same house. One of these business men live just outside town so this is the house I want to gather them together at. This house is owned by a man named Kevin Gretchen and he is one of the business men that told to save his own skin with the law," I stated.

It was a little past midnight and it was about time to get to work. I went into my bedroom, opened the closet, took out a large duffel bag, and carried it out to the front family room. I pulled out three untraceable hand guns and handed them to the men that will help me tonight. I also gave them a pair of gloves so we didn't leave fingerprints and I gave them each a rubber mask that looked like a face so no one could identify us.

When it was time to leave, I told the two other mafia men, "Okay men, it is dark out so we can get this dirty job done. We will take my car to Kevin's place to start the job that I have worked out in my head. I think it's a well thought out idea to assassinate these men in a way we don't get caught."

We piled into my wife's automobile then I started the engine and backed onto the street. I decided to take my wife's vehicle since it would be hard for us to all fit into my truck. It took almost thirty minutes to drive to the other edge of town were our first victim lived. We know each one of these men has a family and we were going to kill all of them as well. We pulled into Kevin's driveway and noticed all the lights were off.

I asked these two, "Who doesn't mind being the man that is going to kill everybody tonight?"

Luke answered back to me and he said, "I don't mind killing anybody over this one."

"The first part of this plan, I want us to kick the door in and have you, Luke, run through the house as fast as possible killing Kevin's whole family, but do not kill Kevin," I explained this part of the plan to Luke.

We got out of the vehicle, quietly approached the front door, and I kicked the door in. Luke went running through the house, first upstairs. We heard two gunshots. The first two shots were Kevin's two children. Luke then came running back downstairs then into Kevin's bedroom. Kevin and his wife were awoken by the front door being kicked in and were now standing and out of bed. There was one more shot and Luke killed Kevin's wife right in front of him. He then approached Kevin and held him at gunpoint.

"Move into the front family room of your home or I will shoot you like I just did to your whole family," Luke spoke in a loud voice.

"You need to know that this is payback time for being a snitch on Paul the Pimp with your other businessman friends," I said to this worthless family man.

Kevin started to cry and asked, "You just shot and killed my children and my wife?"

"Yes, we did do that. So now you see what happens if you rat on professional criminals," Luke answered.

"Travis, I am making it your job to watch this man here at his house while we go and get the other five men that told on Paul to save their skin with the law," I instructed to Travis.

Travis asked this businessman, "What type of deal did you get with the government for snitching on Paul?"

"Five years in prison instead of ten is what the police expected, but I don't know because I haven't been in court yet, not even a hearing," he answered.

"Luke, this is what we are going to do at every one of these businessmen's homes," I explained. "We will kick the door in and kill the whole house except for the man who snitched. After we do a family in, we will drive that businessman over here immediately and then drive out to get another one. Travis here will watch them at gunpoint and make sure they don't get away. I told Travis this is his job."

We left to go round up the other of the men who decided they would tell on Paul to get themselves out of this situation they had with the law. Every one of these men spent the trip from their house crying because we killed their whole family and they fear us. Every time we showed up at this house with one of these rats that Travis was guarding, we had to hear them beg for their lives and we would hear Travis telling them to shut up.

"Gentlemen, us mafia men have gathered you here for a reason," I said. "That reason is because the Godfather that is in charge of all mafia is upset with you and so are we. We can do this the easy way or the hard way, it depends on how much pain you want there to be with your death." I asked the room, "Raise your hand if you would rather be tortured to death rather than shot painlessly?

"Okay, it looks like no one raised their hand which is what we want," Luke exclaimed. "Since, this is Kevin's house, we will let him do the honors before your untimely demise.

"Kevin, I want you to be the man of the evening that writes the suicide note for the room. Write, as I speak," I said to Kevin. "We have recently encountered problems with the government. We are men condemned to prison for child prostitution, because of this we have decided to take our own lives and the lives of our families. By the time you read this note, our families will be dead and so will we. Goodbye."

"Now that Kevin has written this note, I want all of you to line up against that wall and turn around so you are no longer facing us, but not you Kevin," Luke spoke.

They lined up sobbing and pleading for their lives but we had no regard for their lives. Five shots later, all these men were shot dead and we hoped we would get away with this. I think we should get away with this if the police believe the suicide note. Now it is Kevin's turn, we pointed the pistol at his temple so it looks like he killed all these men and their families. He then turned the gun at himself and blew his own brains out.

We were done here. We then drove back to my place and all intended on drinking to forget what we just did. Killing grown men that ticked us off was one thing but women and children was a completely different idea.

Chapter 9

It had been about a month since Paul was arrested and about the same amount of time since we executed the men that told on him for selling child prostitutes. We had noticed that the law wasn't watching us as close as they were. My potion cook was back in business and Paul the Pimp was not back in business since he received fifteen years for good behavior and thirty for bad behavior. It really did matter that Paul was not around anymore because he would do whatever it takes if it was something that needed done. I had made a visit to my secret storage garage, then I gave Robby his potion equipment back and I got my potion back so I could start making money selling potion again.

I heard a knock at the door. It was Luke from the job we did together for Paul the Pimp. He was sent to my house by the Godfather to introduce me to the man he was with. The man's name was Gary Toothman. Luke had a story about him and why I need to know him. Luke was with him so I could be told that I could trust him.

Gary stretched out his right hand to shake mine and then said, "Hello my name is Gary."

I replied with, "Hi my name is Rick Thompson. What can I do for you gentlemen today?"

Gary said, "I sell potion in a city called Stanworth and my potion expert decided to get caught and went to prison."

Luke asked me, "Do you think it will be worth your time to personally ship two hundred thousand doses of potion to his place in Stanworth?"

I answered by saying, "Yes, it will cost two-hundred thousand dollars exactly because potion is one dollar per dose in large amounts. However, it is two dollars per dose in small amounts."

Luke mentioned, "We have a man that is being taught how to make potion in Stanworth but he is not good enough at it yet and we want potion in town now."

I said to them, "I know where Stanworth is. It is about two weeks by automobile and I will have to find a vehicle that will ship this much potion. I know I can rent a moving van that will hold this big of a shipment but I will have to make sure I don't get pulled over," I told them. "When do you want this shipment to arrive at your place Gary?"

He answered, "I would like it in town within about a month."

"You're going to have to give me about two weeks to give my supplier the time to mix up a batch this size," I told Gary. Then I also said, "It will take me two weeks to get it to where you are at." I asked, "If I bring you this much potion, can I be assured that you will have this much cash to pay me?"

He answered with "Yes, I have that kind of money to spend. It will not be a problem when you show up with the merchandise."

"Why don't we drive to Robby's house right now and make sure he can come up with this much product," I told them both.

Luke spoke up with, "We can take my vehicle if you want then we can drop you off at home on our way out of town."

"We will have to hope he is home because it doesn't look like he is since there are no lights on even though its daylight," I stated to these two mafia men while we knocked on the door. The door opened and as it did I said, "Hello Robby, can we come in and talk some business?"

Robby replied with, "Yes, that would be fine. I always want business being done over here."

"I wasn't sure if you were home or not since there were no lights on," I told Robby.

Robby said back, "I was in the basement working, what do you men want?"

"This man, whose name is Gary, wants to buy two hundred thousand doses worth of potion," I told Robby. "I am over here to ask you how long it will take for you to have this large of an order."

Robby said, "I have about ten thousand doses right now so I will need to come up with another one-hundred and ninety-thousand doses. This will take about fifteen days, I predict."

I asked Robby politely, "Can you make sure you have this amount of potion within the next two weeks?"

Robby answered, "I will do my best."

"If Robby gets this one done in about two weeks, I will do my best to get your merchandise to you as fast as I can," I explained to Gary.

Gary replied with, "That sounds fine with me. Lets drop you back off at home so we can leave town."

"Goodbye, have a good trip and I will see you in Stanworth as soon as I can," I said to Luke and Gary as I exited their automobile.

I was waiting for Robby to have the potion ready for me to bring to Stanworth and sell to Gary Toothman. In the meantime, I was selling potion out of my house in smaller amounts.

While I was doing business out of my home, I got a visit from Jennifer Nicolson, who used to be Paul's most popular prostitute. Now that Paul was in the big house, Jennifer had no work. So she showed her face over here and said, "I will run out of money soon because Paul, who is my boss, is in prison."

Jennifer, whom I had assumed wanted to buy some potion, had a different reason for being here.

After I Let Jennifer into my home she asked, "Since Paul who was my boss is now in prison, how would you like to run all of Paul's girls as our new manager?"

I replied to her saying, "I don't know if this is something I want to do or not." I also told her, "I keep plenty busy selling potion and I would always have to make time for this."

She pleaded to me, "Please decide you can manage all of us girls so we can start making money again."

I asked, "How many girls did Paul manage besides you?"

She answered, "There are thirty-five of us that Paul took care of. Paul said if we can find some to replace him, he will teach them how to do his job during visitation at the prison he is in."

"I will go talk to Paul in prison during visitation and find out what this job takes but I am not promising you anything," I said to Jennifer.

Jennifer then asked, "Could I buy five doses of potion from you while I am here?"

"Sure, let me run downstairs into my basement and I will be right back," I told Jennifer. As I came back up the stairs I said to Jennifer, "Here you are" as I handed her the potion and told her, "This will be ten dollars."

"Let me rummage through my purse and... okay, here is ten dollars," she said as she handed it to me.

"I will let myself out Rick, think about what I asked you and get back to me as soon as possible," Jennifer stated as she left out the front door.

I decided I would consider Jennifer's offer of managing her and her little co-workers. The day after Jennifer asked me to be a pimp and not only a sup-plier of fine goods, I decided to go to the prison and talk to Paul. I know I can usually do bad things even if it gets at my conscience a little bit. I was thinking this as I walked into the prison to see Paul during visitation hours.

"Hi Paul," I said to him, as I sat down on a small steel table in the prison's visitation room. "Jennifer Nicolson stopped by my place the other day and she was looking for me to take over your business with the women of the night."

Paul asked, "Are you thinking about doing this for them, the women I mean?"

"It depends on how much time it is going to take me to do this on the side from my potion business," I told Paul. I was pretty much asking Paul to teach me how to be a pimp and so I said, "I was hoping that you could tell me how to be a pimp and maybe I will have the time to take over your business."

"There is not much to it actually, you just have to be brave enough to get in some confrontations with other men," Paul explained. "First, have the girls explain how much they charge. Never bend this for any customer. It does matter which girl is charging because of the quality of the girl," Paul said this was key. "The girls go out at night to pick up men that want a good time, they know how much to charge and I would recommend that you don't change this," Paul instructed.

"As long as everybody pays for the service, just leave all of your customers alone and you will have customers that are regulars. The hard part of the job is getting customers to pay up when they don't want to. You will have to go bad on customers that didn't pay so you can make death threats, give beatings, or even kill someone that just wouldn't pay," Paul said was the bad part of the job. "For the most part though the girls do all the work, just wait for them to show up in the morning after they wake up and they will have the money they made the night before," Paul said. "When they show up in the morning or early afternoon, you can keep fifty percent of what they made and then give them the rest," Paul exclaimed.

"This is why this job is easy. The worst part is when a man goes bad on one of your employees, maybe he pushes them around or worse beats her senseless," Paul said this in a little more serious voice. He told me, "When this happens always beat the man almost dead so no one gets the idea you allow this behavior in a customer. That is everything you need to be able to do, so it is not a hard job." Paul ended this conversation with the bell that meant visitation is now over and said, "Goodbye and come visit me anytime."

On my way home, driving in my truck, I was still trying to decide if I want to take up Paul's pimping business. If I take the job, I had to worry about going to jail for beating customers if they decide to get on my bad side by not treating the ladies very well. I will have to talk to the girls, find out how much they charge, and how much they work. I am normally interested in new illegal business deals but this one had its own problems and that is the need to be somewhat violent, on the girl's behalf, of course.

It was about three weeks after Paul had been busted when Robby had come to my home and said, "I have two hundred thousand doses of potion created. I forgot how much potion you said you needed."

I said, "two hundred thousand doses". I told Robby, "Do not sell any of it to anyone and I will buy that exact amount for fifty percent."

Robby agreed to this sale and I bought two hundred thousand doses for one hundred thousand dollars.

I had been driving for almost two weeks and as I was getting close to Stanworth I saw flashing lights behind me. It was the police and I don't know where he came from on this desolate road. Now I was nervous, knowing I have a large batch of potion in the back of this moving van, and it is making me rather uneasy to speak with the police officer. As I looked around the countryside, I noticed there is no one that could see me do something that maybe I shouldn't do. With that thought, I placed a small handgun in the back of my pants and then I let my shirt cover it up.

As the police officer walked up to my driver's side window, he said, "Good afternoon and do you know why I pulled you over?"

I answered the officer with, "No, I don't know why I am being stopped."

He said, "You have a tail light out. Do you mind opening up the back of your moving van so I can take a look at what you are hauling?"

"I do actually have a time schedule to keep, is it possible just to let me go with just a warning?"

He turned a little sour at me thinking I might have something to hide if I won't just cooperate. The police officer said, "No, I want to see what is in the back of your truck because now I think you are hiding something you don't want me to see."

"Fine, I will get out and unlock the back of the moving van so you can see inside of it." I started to open my driver's side door and the police officer started walking to the back of my truck. Once I had both feet on the ground, I pulled out the handgun that was inside the back of my pants, pointed it at the back of his head, pulled the trigger, and shot the police officer dead.

I took another look around and I could see that there was no one around to witness what I had just done. I opened the police vehicle's driver's side door. I turned off the flashing lights and popped the trunk open. I picked up the now lifeless policeman, stowed his body in the trunk of his vehicle, and shut the trunk. I then proceeded to get back into my moving van and continued my way to Stanworth. As I pulled into Stanworth, I looked at the address I had written down for Gary Toothman and continued to his home.

Here I am, I thought to myself. I was looking at Gary's address on the front of his house as I pulled into his driveway. Gary's home was quite a bit larger than most people's homes which was how I could tell the potion business is as good as it to him as it is to me. Gary happened to be sitting in front of his house smoking a cigar. I could tell he didn't recognize me until I stepped out of the moving van and starting walking towards him.

Gary waved and asked me, "Who are you? I don't think I know you from anywhere."

I answered back, "My name is Rick Thompson from Greens City. You were at my home about a month ago wanting me to bring you potion since you were having a hard time procuring some in the city you live in."

"Okay, that's right. I hadn't forgotten about that but I had forgotten your face since we only met briefly."

"What I remember was your potion cook had been busted and so you don't have a way to get potion in this city," I exclaimed. "You told me you have someone learning how to brew up the stuff but he is not able to actually make it yet," I said to Gary. "Has the new cook learned how to successfully make the product you sell yet?"

Gary answered, "Not yet, he is still being taught the chemistry that is involved with creating the potion but he has not been taught how to get away with it yet."

"I brought you two hundred thousand doses of potion and you promised to pay me one dollar per dose," I told Gary. "Are you still interested in paying two hundred thousand dollars for this much potion?"

He said, "That sounds like a good deal for me. At one dollar per dose, I can sell it for two dollars per dose and double my money."

I asked Gary, "Where are we going to be unloading all of these commodities and in a way that we won't get seen?"

"We can pull this moving van into my garage, close the garage door, and unload it in to the house," Gary answered. "We will go through the door that is in the garage that lets us into the house," Gary stated. He did say, "I want twenty-five thousand doses in my house and this is how we can get it there but I want the rest at my lake house out of town."

Gary opened his garage door to let the truck in and because of how low the door in the garage is, I backed the truck into the garage. It was a tight fit between the top of the garage door and the moving truck but I eventually fit the truck into the garage. Now that we had the truck in the garage, we shut the garage door, opened the back door of the truck, and unloaded twenty-five thousand doses. I then closed the door to the moving truck, opened the garage door up again, and pulled the truck out of the garage. I parked the truck on the street so his wife will be able to put her car in the garage when she gets home.

It was nice of Gary to let me stay in his home until I could drive home in a few days. Tomorrow, we would be going to his lake house to unload the rest of the potion there and the day after that I would drive back home. It was probably worth it to drive this far because I can make about one-hundred thousand dollars.

We were having lunch at about one o'clock in the afternoon when Gary got a knock at the door from a customer that hadn't seen any decent potion in a while and you could tell he was hard up right now. In fact, Gary had not been able to supply any potion in a while and now he has something to sell his customers.

"Hello Stuart," Gary said to the man, after he let him into the house, knowing that he probably wants to buy potion.

Gary introduced me to Stuart and Stuart asked, "Have either of you seen any potion around?"

Gary answered, "I do have some potion to sell right now, about how much do you want to buy?"

Stuart said, "I want forty dollar's worth of whatever you are selling."

Gary told him, "That will give you twenty doses total."

Stuart then asked, "How about thirty doses of potion for this price because I am a good customer and always have been."

"No way," Gary said to Stuart, "The price is two dollars per dose and that is final."

"Come on man, help me out just this one time and to make up for not having what I needed recently," Stuart begged.

"I will only sell you the twenty doses for forty dollars no matter what," Gary told him.

"Alright fine, it's a deal. I want forty dollar's worth anyways." Gary walked into a spare bedroom, grabbed what his customer wanted, walked out of the bedroom, and handed Stuart his potion saying, "Here you are, that will be forty dollars."

Stuart reached into his back pocket, pulled out his wallet, and handed Gary two twenty-dollar bills and said, "Here you are."

"Also go ahead and tell everybody who buys from me that I am back in business, for a while anyways," Gary told his customer.

In the morning, after everybody was awake, Gary and I went to take the potion that was still in the moving van to Gary's lake house. When we walked outside, I noticed the back door to the van was open a little and I wondered why. I opened the door all the way and noticed that about fifty thousand doses were missing.

I turned to Gary and said, "Some of our potion is missing and I want to know who took it."

"The only person that was here that could know where it might have gone was Stuart," Gary said. "If you remember meeting him yesterday when I sold him some potion, maybe he knows where it might have been taken to," Gary exclaimed.

"Alright, do you know where Stuart lives so we can go talk to him about it?"

"Yes, I do know where he lives and if he didn't take the potion then he might know who did," Gary answered in a voice that was more than a little angry. "Let's get into my automobile and try to track this one down instead of driving your rental van around."

That isn't a bad idea, I thought.

"First, we will try Stuart's place and if he lies to me I am not going to be very happy," Gary stated.

I asked Gary, "Do you think he would steal from you since you clearly have known him for a while?"

"I would put it up to some of his associates that he uses potion with instead of Stuart himself," Gary answered. "This blue house on the right that I am going to stop at is Stuart's house. Let's walk up to Stuart's place, knock on the door, and see what he can tell us," Gary spoke in a solemn voice.

Gary knocked on the door. It opened and both Gary and I said, "Hello."

Gary asked Stuart, "Can we please come in and talk to you Stuart?"

He opened the door all the way and told us, "Come on in if you need to."

There were about five people here. They did not live in this house and clearly they had plenty of potion because of the way they seemed. I was looking around the house for signs of them having too much potion and by that I mean more than Gary sold Stuart. I thought the amount of potion Stuart had bought from Gary should be about gone by now.

"You were at my house yesterday buying potion from me and I want to know who you told I have potion," Gary spoke to Stuart.

"Just these people that are here right now using the potion I bought yesterday," Stuart answered.

"Well, somebody stole a whole bunch of potion out of the back of his moving van and I think you men have something to do with it," Gary exclaimed.

We both could tell that a skinny little retard on the edge of the couch was now a bit uneasy.

Gary pulled a gun on him and said, "I think you may have done this one Samuel. Let's make a little trip to your place and see what we can find," Gary yelled.

Samuel replied by saying, "I am kind of busy right now, so how about you come by my place tomorrow and we can do this then?"

Gary asked rhetorically, "Why, so you can get rid of what I think you might have stolen from us?"

Samuel answered, "No, I am just kind of intoxicated right now and so I don't want to have to stand up."

"Too bad Samuel, get off the couch and let's go to your place right now," Gary stammered.

"I am not going anywhere," Samuel said while fearing Gary and the pistol he had in his right hand.

"If you don't get up and come with me right now, I will shoot you in both knee caps and drag you back to your place bleeding to death," Gary threatened.

"No way. I am not going anywhere with you Gary and you're going to stop pointing that gun at me," Samuel shouted.

"Just grab a hold of the little nut-job Rick and drag him kicking and screaming out to the backseat of my automobile," Gary said to me.

That is precisely what I did since he may have been guilty of stealing my potion that also belongs to Gary. I picked him up, he didn't weigh much, probably because of the potion he seems to have taken a liking to. Like a sack of potatoes, I hauled his gimpy body back out to the vehicle and crammed him into the back seat. Both Gary and I climbed into the front two seats of the automobile, backed out onto the street, and then started towards Samuel's place.

I asked Gary, "Do you know where he lives at here in town?"

"Yes, I do know where he lives. He lives in a small suburb full of high-end apartment buildings called Bush Heights," Gary answered.

I then asked Gary, "What are we going to do with this little thief, if we find our potion at his home?"

"If he did steal, I am going to beat him almost to death, take the potion back home, and not deal with him anymore."

We pulled up into a small parking lot that belonged to this large brick apartment complex called Bush Heights. Gary and I got out of his vehicle, then I pulled Samuel out of the back seat and Gary motioned for us to follow him.

"This is the place and his apartment is on the top floor with the apartment number 506," Gary told us.

"You first Samuel, we will follow you, since it is your home were walking up to," I said to the possible thief.

Once we were in front of Samuel's apartment door, he reached into his front pocket, pulled out a set of keys, and unlocked the door. At first glance, there was no sign of potion anywhere in his apartment but we figured he probably had it hiding somewhere. We started to go through his home looking for it. First, we looked in the kitchen and there was nothing to be found, even in his full-size pantry. Next, we tried the living room and it wasn't under any furniture or even in the broom closet. The last place to look was in the bedroom. There wasn't anything under the bed and the last place it could be hiding at was in the bedroom walk-in closet. I opened the door to his closet and there it was, piled up against the back of the closet.

I asked Samuel, "How do you explain all the potion that you have hiding in your closet?"

He answered, "Someone made me hide it there or they were going to kill me. I don't even know where they got it from."

"I do not believe that horrible lie of yours," I exclaimed to Samuel.

"Well it's true and you can't take it or they might do something really bad to me, that's if it goes missing. I am telling you the truth."

Is this what Samuel is trying to get by us?

"That is just too bad for you then, because we are going to take all of it back," Gary told Samuel.

He did have a large suitcase in his closet and I said to Gary, "Let's use the suitcase that is in there to load up one trip at a time out to your automobile. This way no one sees us carrying potion out across the parking lot."

Now, that we had all the potion in Gary's backseat and trunk, Gary went walking back up to the thief's apartment and opened the door. We then walked in, he pointed the gun at Samuel and started slamming the handgun handle into his head and face. Once Samuel was on the ground, Gary kicked him the face and stomach about ten times each. After he was unconscious and bleeding profusely out his nose, we left the apartment and drove back to Gary's place. I was kind of thinking that he might die since he was bleeding so much, but if that's what happens to him, then that's what he gets for robbing us.

We were now back at Gary's place and we had gotten all the stolen potion back from the thief known as Samuel. We spent the night drinking after a play we went and saw that was playing here in town for about the last two weeks. After we had enough drinks at a local pub, we went back to Gary's place by taxi and fell asleep for the night.

Today was the day I was planning on leaving Stanworth to drive home to Greens City. I would be leaving town about now but since we got robbed I had to wait until today to bring Gary's potion to his lake house. In the early afternoon, Gary and I hopped into my moving van and drove it out to his lake house. When we arrived at his lake house, we unloaded all the potion into his lake house's basement. He put a padlock onto the basement door so no one could just let themselves down into his basement. Later that night, we went out to eat at an Italian restaurant then went back to Gary's and listened to the radio until we fell asleep for the night.

I was on the road the next day, driving the rental moving van back to Greens City. On the way there, I had to make sure that I did not get pulled over because I had illegal goods in the vehicle. On the way home, I did not have this problem because Gary had bought all the potion I had driven there with. I decided, since I didn't have anything illegal in the truck, I would break the law and speed just so I could get home a little faster.

Chapter 10

The next day after I had arrived at home, I decided I would try and spend the day with my wife because I had not seen her in a few days. We were both relaxing in the front family room with a little whiskey and our children were at school. It was early in the afternoon when I received a knock at the door. I figured this was normal because it is probably someone wanting to buy my products. When I opened the door, I saw Jennifer Nicolson standing in front of me. I opened the door and let her into my home. I was guessing she wanted potion.

I asked Jennifer with a smile, "Hello, what can I do for you today Jennifer?"

She replied with a question of her own, "Have you decided to take over Paul's business of managing us girls or have you decided not to take over his business?"

"I had talked to Paul in jail about what this business takes," I mentioned to Jennifer. "So if I that I have the time to sell potion and do Paul's job at the same time, then I will give this business a try," I explained. This is what I said to Jennifer about managing her and her friends; when she brought this up a few weeks ago. I then told her, "I decided that I would take the job and see how it goes after looking over a schedule I set up to decide if I do have the free time."

I had just woken up for the day, it was about eight-thirty in the morning, and so I started getting ready for the day. After finishing my one pot of coffee I drink every morning, and saying goodbye to my children on their way to school, I got in the shower, bathed, shaved, and got dressed for the day. That's when I got another visit from Jennifer.

When I opened the door to Jennifer, she was crying and claimed, "One of my co-workers named Shelly Goldstein was stabbed last night by a customer."

I asked, "Where is she right now?"

She answered, "Right now she is in the hospital and she is not answering the police's questions. She doesn't want to answer the police because prostitution is illegal and she doesn't want the police to know she is a prostitute," Jennifer sort of wept as she spoke. "Shelly told the police that she was on her way to the liquor store to buy a bottle of vodka when she was attacked in the parking lot of a liquor store. The man that attacked her only lived about one block from the liquor store and her automobile was also parked right by the liquor store," Jennifer continued to tell me. "She told them this story because it made sense that she was only going to the liquor store."

I told Jennifer just to wait one minute, I would get my keys to my automobile and then we could drive to the hospital. Once I found my keys, Jennifer and I drove down to the hospital to see one of my new employees. We walked in to the hospital's front doors and up to the front desk.

I asked the receptionist at the front desk, "Where can we find Shelly Goldstein's room?"

She told us, "Walk straight down this hall to the emergency room and she is at the end of the hall past the emergency room."

"Thank you very much, we will walk down this hall and try to find her," I said.

As Jennifer and I walked into Shelly's room, she greeted her friend with a groggy, "Hello Jennifer and who is this man that is with you?"

She answered her question by saying, "This is Rick. He is going to take over Paul's business so he will be managing us girls. I told all of you girls, he will be taking care of us now that Paul is in jail but I still have not introduced anybody to him yet."

Shelly greeted Rick with, "Hello to my new boss and hopefully you can make sure that this kind of thing that happened to me doesn't happen all the time."

"I will do my best to keep you safe as this is part of the job," I answered back. Then I asked, "On that note, who did this to you and where can I find him?"

"He is a regular of mine named Craig Wellson. He lives at 516 Ridge Road and he has never done something like this before," she answered.

"This will be my first job after taking over for Paul. I will go down to his house. I am going to shoot him in one knee cap and make sure it probably doesn't kill him," I assured Shelly. "Maybe I should meet with all you girls sometime soon so that way I know all your names and faces," I told both these girls.

"I can tell them to be at your place tomorrow night, if that would be soon enough," Jennifer stated.

I told her, "That would be soon enough. Let's say maybe sometime around eight o'clock in the evening."

After the conversation I had with Shelly, I left with Jennifer, and we drove back to my place in my truck. When we got back, she got into her automobile and drove home. I was going to grab a handgun, go over to the man's house that beat up one of my new girls, and give him a lesson on how to treat a woman.

About an hour later, I drove my truck over to Craig Wellson's house, walked up to his door, and banged on the door as hard as I could.

After I banged on the door, a man the other side, while looking through the peephole, asked, "Who is it?"

I answered back by saying, "My name is Rick and I want to talk to a Craig Wellson if he is available."

The man then asked, "Are you the government or the police?"

"No, I am not the law and I won't be making an arrest on anyone."

The door opened and the man on the other side introduced himself by saying, "My name is Craig, what can I do for you today?"

I stepped into his house, pulled out the handgun I had in a holster under my jacket, pointed it at him, and motioned for him to sit down on his leather sofa. Once he sat down, I took a seat across from him on a recliner and I started talking to him. I was frowning at this man when I started to talk to him and this made him start to cry.

"First, I should start by introducing myself. My name is Rick and I am a mafia man," I announced.

He asked me, "What do you need with me?"

I answered his question with one of my own. "Do you know a woman named Shelly Goldstein?"

"The name sounds familiar," he replied.

"I should think the name sounds familiar because you almost killed her last night in a knife attack," I stammered.

"Yeah, well, why does it matter you? This is Paul's problem not yours," he shrieked. Then he stated, "Since Paul is in jail right now, he doesn't have a way to do anything about it so I did what I wanted to the little whore."

"You are right, Paul can't do anything about it but I took over his business now that he is locked up," I stated to him in a firm voice.

"Well then, you don't get to do anything about it since I didn't know she had a new pimp," he claimed in a sour voice.

"Okay, that is the first time I have ever been called a pimp. I hate that but I am going to do something about this anyways," I scoured as I told him this. I then pointed my gun at his right knee, pulled the trigger, and shot him in the leg. The pain from the gunshot made him scream. "That is what I will do about this for the first time, but if I have to come back I will be aiming for the chest!" I yelled.

I let myself out of his home, now that I made him pay, climbed into my truck, and drove home. I had just thought to myself, *Do I have anything else to do today?* The only thing I could come up with is I had to meet all my new employees tomorrow night. When I got home, I just relaxed for the rest of the day, listened to the radio, and answered the door to some of my regulars that wanted to buy potion.

Later in the evening, the day after my visit with Shelly in the hospital, I heard a knock at the door. When I opened it there stood about thirty-five women. Every one of these women that I was letting in my front door had almost no clothes on. I think I could have enjoyed these women a lot more if my wife wasn't at home. Speaking of my wife, she scoured and told the children to go to their bedrooms for the night when she noticed what these women of the night were wearing. After they were all inside my home, some of them had to stand because I didn't have enough places for all thirty-five of them to sit.

"Alright ladies, now that you are all here we can start," I told the room.

"The point here is for all of us to get to know our new employer Rick, that is him over there," Jennifer said to the room as she pointed at me. "His last name is Thompson and people that know him call him, Rick 'The Slick Man' Thompson."

One of the women in the room asked, "How much do you know about the pimping business because Paul was actually really good at it."

I claimed, "I actually don't know much about this business other than what Paul told me from his jail cell."

"Then you have a lot to learn, so you don't lose us money or decide to wimp out of dangerous situations that we can get ourselves in," one of the other women chimed in.

"I will not ever wimp out because I have been a potion salesman for a long time so I know what it takes to sit on the wrong side of the law." I did mean this and I know I won't wimp out. "I do know this part of the job and that is defending all of you. So if you have problems, you need to know my door is always open," I told the crowd. "I do want as little violence as possible on all of you women so events like last nights attack on Shelly do not happen if we can help it," I said in a loud voice so they knew to try and keep this from happening to them.

I then told them, "Just so you know, when you show up at my place for any reason at all I want you to be fully clothed if you can help it. The reason I want you to cover up at my place is because I have small children that I am raising."

One of the women spoke up and said, "My name is Katrina Brown and I have an issue that maybe you can fix for me. Last night a man kicked me out of his house and refused to pay for the service."

I asked her, "Do you remember what his address and name are?"

Katrina answered, "Yeah, I know where he lives at and even where he works since he has requested me more than one time."

"Tell me who he is and give me his address before you leave tonight," I told Katrina. "Tomorrow afternoon, maybe after he gets off work, I will go over to his house and collect your payment. The one thing I wanted to do is take all your pictures with this camera," I explained. "I also want all of you to write down your name as well as your address in this notebook I have on the table," I spoke loudly enough for all of them to hear everything I said.

I had them all line up, in a single file line and had them write in the notebook the information I had just requested from them. I also snapped a picture of each one of them. I had to make sure I remember to get them developed as soon as I can. After I had documented who these women are and how to find them, they left for the night.

Before Katrina left she told me the name of the man who ripped her off. "Jason Smith is his name and his address is 229 Pine St."

I hadn't done much but sit around and wait forthe man who ripped off Katrina to finish his day at work. I wanted to go over and make him pay up as soon as possible. I did have a good day of selling potion out of my house. I made over six-thousand dollars in one day, I usually consider one-thousand dollars in a day productive. It is about five thirty now and I was going to get into my truck to drive over to Jason's house to ask him why he gets our services for free.

I noticed as I walked up to Jason's front door that he has the money to pay me for the other night. I could see him watching me from his front window as I walked up his driveway. The door opened before I got all the way up his driveway and Jason stepped out through his front door. He waved and greeted me as I finished walking up to him.

"Hello, my name is Rick," I stated as I walked up to him. Then I asked, "Is your name Jason?"

He replied, "Yes, my name is Jason Smith. What can I do for you today?"

I asked Jason this question, "I was wondering if we could go inside and talk about something that has been bothering me?"

"If that is what you need from me, I would be pleased to have a guest over," he answered. "Just follow me in and you can have a seat on one of my to easy chairs or the sofa if that would be more comfortable," Jason instructed.

I then asked him another question. "Do you know a woman named Katina Brown who was over here a couple of nights ago?"

"The name sounds familiar but I am having a hard time remembering a face," he said back to me in a manner that sounded like he was lying and he knows exactly who she is.

"Well then, I will refresh your memory. She is a prostitute that was over here that you had done business with and then failed to pay her," I exclaimed.

Then Jason asked his question. "Why do you care if I don't pay some tramp for a night because last I knew Paul, her pimp, was in prison?" He then added, "So I don't know why you need to come over here and bother me about it."

"I am her new manager now that Paul is in prison. I want payment for what she did for you the other night or we are going to have some problems," I scolded him with the tone of my voice while I told him to pay up.

"It's news to me that there is a new pimp in town which is why maybe I should have given Katrina the money I owed her when she was over here," Jason admitted.

I asked him "Are you going to pay up and give me the money you owe Katrina and me?"

"Yes, I will pay you the money I owe because I don't want problems with someone like you," Jason claimed as he reached for his wallet in his back pocket. "Here is the money I should have paid the other night for what Katrina did over here," He stammered this out while he handed me the cash.

"Good, I am glad we took care of this the easy way so there isn't anything messy happening over here tonight," I told Jason.

After this I drove home in my truck, on the way I stopped by Katrina's house and paid her the money Mr. Smith didn't pay her like he should have. When I got home, I spent the rest of the night with a bottle of scotch, the radio, and customers who wanted potion.

Chapter 11

Bang! Bang! Bang! I heard at my door early this morning along with, "Open up, it's the police."

As I was getting out of bed, I then heard a crash that was my door being kicked in. The police came running through my house. Before they made it to my bedroom I had looked out the window. That's when I saw about thirty government and police vehicles. Along with the cars I saw about fifty or so government employees with local police. I had to start thinking about what I didn't get away with. The police eventually made it into my bedroom and tackled me, not to mention scare my wife half to death. The police put the handcuffs on, probably little too tight for my liking. They then stood me up and escorted me out into the back of a paddy wagon. When we made it down to the cities public jail, I was told I was responsible for the murder of Eleanor Wilson. I know I remember doing it quite a while back and I did it for Paul the Pimp's friend who was a thief by trade. There was no way I am going to admit to anything yet. The police sat me down in a small interrogation room and then about five minutes later a local crime investigator joined.

The investigator said, "We think you have recently broken the law and we want you to tell us about it."

I replied with, "What is it that you believe I have done exactly?"

"Well, we want you to tell us what you think you have done," the investigator remarked.

I exclaimed back, "I am not playing those games with you Investigator… wait, what is your name?"

"I am Investigator Mark Patron, if that is what you are asking," he stuttered out.

I know he can't play those games with me. "I am not telling you anything I have done until you tell me what you think I have done," I stammered back.

"Very well," the investigator said, "Let's do it your way. I and the rest of the police on this case believe you have murdered Eleanor Wilson."

Of course, since I am a mafia man that intends on not getting caught, I lied right through my front teeth. I told him, "I don't know this person that was murdered and I have never murdered anyone." I wanted to know what evidence they had on me before I lied too much so I knew what I was lying about. I then asked the next question, "I want to know what evidence you have on me before I am willing to talk about anything and I want to talk to my lawyer."

Mark claimed, "There is no evidence but there is a witness that claims you actually killed this woman for him. The man that claims you killed Eleanor Wilson for him is named Stan Somersworth. Stan had an interesting story why you did this for him, not to mention the money you were paid to do it," the investigator explained. "He was on trial for a crime, the crime was murder and there was no evidence," Mark continued to explain. "Stan happened to be robbing a man's house and no one was home. The man who owned this home had gotten off work early that day and caught Stan robbing him."

As the investigator told me, this I realized I didn't know how he had gotten caught in the first place.

"According to Stan, this started a fight when the owner of the house attacked him for breaking in and Stan ended up killing this man in self-defense," the investigator continued to tell me how this actually went. He then explained, "We actually had no evidence on him right away, but after we combed the area we found a knife dropped into a rain gutter with Stan's fingerprints and the other man's blood. We had a witness to the case, her name was Eleanor Wilson, and this is who you are being accused of killing," Mark spoke in a low, serious voice. "We believe you killed this woman so she could not testify to what she saw Stan doing at her neighbor's house."

"Is this all you have on me is what this Stan said and he couldn't even claim he saw me do it? If this is it and you don't have a real eye witnesses or any actual evidence, then you have no case and I want to leave now or talk to my lawyer," I stated firmly.

"Fine, have it your way, deny that you may have done this. We are going to bring up charges and try to prove it in court. Let him call his lawyer since he requested it and it is the law that we have to let him," the investigator told another officer.

I called my lawyer whose name is Chance Billard. I explained the murder charge the police have brought me up on. It was about twenty minutes later when my lawyer showed up.

Chance and Mark shook hands then greeted each other with a "Hello."

My lawyer asked the first question, "What are the charges and what is the evidence?"

The investigator claimed, "Murder is what we have him here for. We do have a witness and we don't have any evidence."

Chance then turned to me and said, "They cannot keep you with such a small amount of evidence." He then turned to Mark and said, "You have no case so you have to let him go and that's because there is no actual evidence."

The investigator replied with, "You're right we can't keep him, but we still are pressing charges based on the witness's testimony."

Chance then explained, "If they want to take you to court for this they actually can, even though they have to let you go for now."

On my way out of the jail that the police brought me to, I was handed a small piece of paper that had a court date on it. The court date was for about three weeks from now. My lawyer drove me home from the city jail and when I got there I had to discuss this with my wife.

After I had told my wife that I had been charged with murder, she said, "I have been unsure about our relationship for a long time. I have thought that I do not know how you never have been caught doing something like this." Then she also said, "It has felt like this to me for a long time and what I mean is no matter what bad things happen, you keep doing whatever you want." She then added, "I think it is time you take a vacation from your career for at least three years."

"I can do this for you if want me to Linda and the good part of this wish of yours is we have the finances to make it without me working," I remarked back to my wife.

My wife wanted me to quit selling potion and not take any criminal jobs from anyone. She wanted me to stop doing my job as a mafia man for at least three years. I had sat around the house for about three weeks and spent some of this time telling my customers that I will not be selling any of my normal products and I cannot be hired for anything illegal, wrong, or immoral.

During the last three weeks, I had nothing to do since I was no longer the salesman I was known to be. I was also brainstorming a way to win in court against the terrible thief Stan who had had snitched on me. The situation I was in happened to be that I had killed a witness for Stan, who is a brilliant thief. I did this so he would not be convicted since the only witness to a murder he committed was now dead. Later, after I had done this, the police proved this murder of Patrick Bensy on Stan. They had found the murder weapon not far from the victim's house. They connected it to him with fingerprints and the victim's blood.

What I knew is that the only evidence or witnesses in my murder case was Stan the thief. The thief Stan claims he paid me to kill someone for him so there would be no witness to convict him. Fortunately for me, Stan didn't have any records that he paid me to off someone for him, he did not see me do it, and so far, there was no evidence that I killed the person I did. I did know that besides Stan's testimony, no one had anything on me in this case unless I slipped up and confessed to this crime, and there was no way I wanted to do that. Right now I know that there is no evidence on me except for Stan. I know I can get rid of this witness so then they can't prove anything. Even though the law will know I killed Stan to get rid of any evidence against me, I will make sure they can't put Stan's murder on me. Therefore, I contacted the Godfather to see what he could do for me and he said he will send someone to clean this up. The big problem is that Stan is protected from us by sitting in prison for murder.

Today, the Godfather was at my house and he told me, "It will cost you fifty thousand dollars to take out Stan in prison." He then asked, "Do you have that kind of money to pay for this service of mine?"

"I will be able to afford this without any problems at all," I answered the Godfather.

"The way this one will go is I have a man that has been jailed for life and he is in the same prison as Stan," the Godfather explained.

"Go on," I said to the Godfather.

"For ten thousand dollars, he will stab Stan to death before your court appearance you have to make in about a week," the Godfather exclaimed.

"Alright, well get it done. I have fifty thousand in a vault in the basement and I can pay you today."

The last thing the Godfather said was, "I am also going to appoint my personal lawyer to take your case." The Godfather left with my payment of fifty thousand dollars in the trunk of his car. He told me right before he left, "Don't you dare snitch me out for having this done or I will take you out."

It was the day of my court date and I had just pulled up in front of the courthouse in my truck. I walked through the front doors, up to my lawyer, and started discussing the evidence against me with him.

I asked him the first question after I walked up to him and said, "What are the chances of me being convicted and what is your name?"

He said, "Well there is no actual physical evidence against you so that is good news for you and my name is Billy Conrad, I am the Godfather's lawyer. There was a witness to the case and he was the man who informed the police you had killed someone for him, but he was killed in prison."

"So," I asked, "If I am getting this right there is no evidence and no witness?"

"That appears to be the whole case that we are being presented with," the lawyer explained.

I asked, "Did the government say why Stan was murdered in prison?"

He answered back, "The man that killed him said that Stan had stolen a package of cigarettes from him and so that's why he did it. It does now appear that having this happen puts you in favor of being innocent, unless you are going to confess to something," the lawyer told me.

If this is all the lawyer knows, then the law must not know any more, I thought to myself. *It appears the government does not know that I had something to do with this, so I will not be questioned in court about this murder.*

Sometimes a real good mafia man like the Godfather can have something like this done in such a way that no one even knows what really happened. I was happy to hear that the law might not have anything on me.

After hearing this, I made my way into the courtroom right behind my lawyer. I then sat down next to him and I had about five minutes until the proceedings started.

"Hear ye, hear ye, the court is now in session," this was spoken loudly by the bailiff.

The judge straightened out the wooden name tag that sat on his desk and then introduced himself by saying, "My name is Judge Troy Williams." The judge then turned to my lawyer and asked, "Is he pleading innocent or guilty?"

I answered the question right away and said, "I am pleading innocent, Judge Williams."

"Okay prosecution, present your case," the judge stated.

The prosecution began with, "We are pushing for murder and we will drop it to a lesser murder charge for a guilty plea today." The prosecuting attorney then added "Will you, Rick Thompson, plead guilty for a lesser conviction?"

I answered with, "No, if you want me guilty then you have to prove it."

The judge then told the prosecution, "Present your evidence."

The prosecution stated, "We have no physical evidence and we had one witness. However, he was murdered in prison so all we have is his testimony."

The judge, then somewhat repeated what the prosecution said, by stating, "So you have no evidence and no actual witness on this case?"

"That is probably correct, but we did have one witness when these charges were filed. However, he is no longer with us," the prosecutor explained. "My name is Jamie Larson, I am the prosecuting attorney and I would like to state what the diseased witness claimed," the lawyer told the courtroom. "Rick Thompson killed a woman that was a witness in Stan Sowersworth's murder case so no one could convict because the only witness is dead."

The judge then replied with a question. "So, as I understand it, you still have no witness and no evidence, is that correct?"

"Yes, this happens to be the case," the prosecutor answered back.

The judge asked my lawyer, "Does the defense have anything else to add?"

"Nothing at the moment, other than I do not understand how this man is on trial when there is no case at all because we have no evidence and no witness."

"It appears to me that this case is not lawful since there is no evidence and no way to legally convict," the judge told the courtroom. "With this lack of evidence on the prosecution's part, I am declaring this case to be closed and find Rick Thompson not guilty in this court of law," the judge explained.

This was good news for me and also good news for my wife since she doesn't want to be raising our children by herself. I know we have plenty of money in the bank from my unlawful salesmanship but she didn't think she could be a homemaker without a man in the house. My wife left our children with a babysitter so they won't see me be taken to court while she watched the proceedings. After I was let go, my wife and I then spent the night at a restaurant then a local drinking establishment to try to let ourselves relax and forget about the stressful day we both had.

Chapter 12

It was now turning into fall. I had an exciting summer but not always the way I had planned with the whole murder case I went through. I was accused of murder and then found not guilty even though I had done the deed. I also lost a friend or two on account of them getting caught or killed, it can end like this for a mafia man. I know that I had told my wife that I would stop being a mafia man for a few years, but there was one last job I wanted to complete. After this one last score, I may even decide to retire completely.

I heard from Robby in the beginning of spring that he had found an entire orchard of wild cherry apple trees. The cherry apple is an extremely potent natural potion and each one of them goes for about twenty dollars apiece. Robby told me where to find these in the beginning of spring and now that it was fall they are probably ready to be harvested.

I recently talked to Robby and he said, "There are cherry apple trees that are growing out of town in the wild. We had talked to each other about this in the spring before we could ever pick them. I will pay you ten dollars apiece for the fruit because I have a way of selling them for fifteen dollars apiece to a traveling potion salesman." The man Robby could sell them to is the man he buys potion ingredients from.

I asked Robby, "Why don't you go out and pick them yourself because you can still sell them for fifteen dollars apiece?"

Robby replied, "I am too afraid of getting caught for harvesting the cherry apples because I am not that good of a mafia man but I am that good of a chemist. I however do dare to sell the fruit to a man I know I can trust, the man I buy potion ingredients from the interesting part about him is that he travels cities in a large conversion van and sells potion ingredients out of it."

It was late at night again and I was planning on harvesting some cherry apples then bring them to Robby's house. He knew to stay up late tonight so he could buy the fruit from me. I was going to do this one last job for Robby and make some quick cash to maybe retire on or just take a break for a few years like my wife asked of me. I had stopped being a mafia man for about the last three to four weeks until I decided to do this one last job, even though my wife wasn't very happy about it.

My wife Linda noticed me being up this late and so she asked, "What are you doing up this late?"

I know I did not tell her what I was going to do with Robby, but I still answered with the truth and told her, "I found a way to make some money really quick, so I am doing one last job for Robby."

"Almost a month ago you told me you were done and now you're already going back to the same old mafia junk," she scolded me with this line.

"This is going to be the last thing I do. It is meant to make one more lump sum of money to live off of while I take a break from my work."

"Okay Rick, I will tell you I am not happy about this one but this better be it," she stammered out. She unhappily asked, "All I want to know is what is the job you have to do so badly and why is it so important?"

I answered back, "I am going to drive out of town over the next few nights to harvest cherry apples and then sell them to Robby for ten dollars apiece."

"If this goes bad Rick, I am not going to just keep forgiving you for any of this anymore," she grumbled out.

I left town to drive out into the country side to where the cherry apple trees were growing. I had filled the back end of my pickup truck with plastic crates to load the fruits into. I was there and there were cherry apples everywhere. Right then I decided I can come out here for a month every night until fall makes the beautiful plants no longer bear this intoxication of money for me and potion for someone else. It took me about an hour to fill up all my crates in the back end of my truck. I then stretched a tarp over the back of my truck so no one, including the law, could see what I was transporting. After I was done I drove back into town and then straight over to Robby's house.

Robby saw my headlights when I pulled up in his driveway. He came outside, walked over to his garage, and opened one of the garage doors from his two-stall garage. After he had the garage door opened, he motioned for me to drive in and this is what I did. After my truck was completely inside the garage, Robby closed the door after me. The next thing I thought was if I could tell whether or not I had been watched or followed. I knew right away that nothing seemed out of the ordinary during my trip across town.

I opened my truck's driver's side door, stepped out, and greeted Robby. "Hello Robby, I have a large shipment for you in the back of my vehicle."

Robby counted out how many cherry apples that I had, then stated, "You have about six- thousand four-hundred dollars' worth of cherry apples in the back of your truck." He told me, "I will be right back with your payment, if you want to join me inside."

Robby walked down a main hallway in his house then he took a left into his guest bedroom. I have stayed in his guest bedroom more than one time. I heard him rustle in the closet for about five minutes then he walked out of the bedroom, up to me, and handed me a stack of one hundred-dollar bills.

I kept up with this destructive task, harvesting natural potions for about two and a half weeks, until Robby seemed like he was acting funny. I asked him "What is your problem? If you have a problem you can tell me what it is because we have been friends for a long time." I couldn't tell if Robby may have been lying to me or not. I wouldn't think Robby would lie to me, but I asked myself if he is lying and what about. I couldn't come up with reason that proved Robby was lying so I simply asked, "You aren't trying to fool me are you Robby?

He said, "No, but I guess I do have a personal problem."

I asked, "Well what is it then? I would like to know what your deal is."

He claimed, "My Aunt Gladson suffered a heart attack and she is in the hospital with a large chance of dying, that is if she has another one."

I believed him after we had this conversation and went home for the rest of the night.

When I awoke in the morning, the first thing I thought about was the problem that Robby was having. My wife knows other married women all over town that she has coffee with quite a bit, so she hears all the gossip.

"Honey," I said to my wife Linda, "You haven't heard any strange news about Robby? That maybe his Aunt Gladson is in the hospital, not doing so well with her health, have you?'

"No, I haven't heard anything new about Robby," She answered. "Why?"

"Oh, no reason," I answered.

It was late that night and all of a sudden I saw headlights coming down the road. They stopped driving and pulled up directly behind my vehicle. The next thing I saw was two red and blue lights flicker on through the woods. Someone stepped out of the automobile that they pulled up in and I knew right away it was the police. The officer walked up to the back of my truck and saw all the cherry apples I had picked that night.

Then the police yelled, "I know you're out there picking cherry apples! Come out with your hands up!"

The first thing I thought was that Robby snitched me out and that is why he was acting funny. I said to myself, *if I get out of this one, Robby is going to pay for it*. I was thinking about what I would do to Robby for being a dirty little rat. What came into my head was that death is in order for Robby. I switched off my flashlight so that way the police couldn't track me through the woods in the dark. I got closer to the officer without leaving the cover of the trees in the dark. I noticed there is only one police vehicle but there were two officers in it. Just in case something happened, I had a loaded handgun located in a holster under my light jacket and I was wearing the jacket to cover up the gun.

My next thought was, *how do I deal with these police officers so I am not arrested tonight?* My first idea was to sneak up on both of them in the dark and get close enough to fire off two lethal shots, killing them both. Then I would cover up the crime so no one could prove it was me then I would be done with harvesting this plant and not come out here anymore.

I got to the edge of the trees, pulled my gun, aimed at the first officer, and shot the first office in the side of the head. I could tell I hit him because of the blood splatter and his head almost blowing up off his shoulders. I then took aim at the second officer and before I could shoot, he ducked behind my truck that they were looking inside of. I had not predicted that he could react so fast and this was probably due to his officer training. Right then, I saw his gun go off and right at that moment I felt a sharpening blow to the chest two times in a row. I had just been shot twice in the chest which made me get woozy. All at the same time, everything went black and I would be a mafia man no more.

Well as you might know, my name is Linda and I was Rick's mafia wife. I know when I married Rick that I could have whatever I wanted because I would always have the money to buy it. There were times with Rick that I regretted being married to him, but it was the choice I had made. With all the money we have in the bank I can continue to live out the rest of my life well off. The only problem now is that I must raise our children without a man in the house. I always knew this day could come and that something dreadful might happen to Rick. Sometimes I don't know how it didn't. The secret though, was Rick knew his job better than you think someone would when it comes to being a mafia man. The story I about Rick and how the people in the mafia really live is something I will probably never tell anyone.

The End